Two's Company

Two Short Stories About Totally Normal People

TC Fitzgerald

For you.

CONTENTS

NOBODY'S HERO

1

The bell above the glass-fronted door tinkled, announcing the arrival of a customer. "Coming!" Carol called from the back room, dropping the file she held onto a stack of reports. She hopped through the open door to her spot behind the front desk, just in time to see the customer straightening to face her. He had been forced to turn sideways and hunch a bit to get through the doorway. Carol smiled with bright-lipstick cheer and perched on her stool. "Welcome to Dark Lord Retirement Agency, how may I help you today?"

The customer shuffled forward—carefully. He was about nine feet tall, four times the width of most people, and seemed tentative with his movements in the tiny office. "Ah," he began, in a horrible, deep, growling voice, "I have a referral?" His eyes were a blazing red and his teeth were all about three inches long and sharp as daggers. The rest of his face, in keeping with these specific features, generally lacked curb appeal.

Carol didn't even bat an eye. She smiled at the monstrous face with the brightest, most encouraging welcome. "Okay! Sounds great! May I scan your referral code?" She picked up the scanner and waited expectantly.

"Sure," the customer growl-grunted, fishing about on his person for a moment. The reason for the delay was primarily his difficulty in locating the pocket-like fold in his black leather outfit. A number of metal spikes and chains attempted to deter him, for the fold wasn't originally designed as a pocket, actually. He had used the strange overlap in the leather as a makeshift pocket, because such high-fashion apparel did not trouble itself with these necessities, and he needed somewhere to put his phone. When he got it out at last, it looked closer to the size of a credit card in his enormous hand. There was a string tied around the phone, attaching it to what seemed to be a pencil. The customer picked it up and stuck the tip of it in his mouth, where he held it for a moment; after this, he took it out, wiped it dry on the back of his other hand, and used it as a stylus to unlock the phone and pull up his QR code. Carol cheerfully scanned the code, still without blinking, even when she saw that the "stylus" was a severed human finger.

Clacking on her keyboard for a moment, she said, "Okay, Mr. Barbaros, you were referred to us by…Skelattack, I see. I'll just credit his account…there. And," she looked cheerfully up at him, "did you have a particular retirement plan in mind, or would you like to see a list of our packages?"

"Uh," Barbaros rumbled, and momentarily scratched at one of his horns. It flaked a little onto the office carpet. "Well, to be honest with you, things are a bit…tight. My budget, I mean. I'm not even sure I can afford to retire, but…" He made a rather hideous expression that was intended for a wince.

Carol's expression immediately clicked over from bright and cheerful to reassuring and confidential. "Oh, no problem at all, Mr. Barbaros. We have a number of exceptionally cost-effective retirement plans designed to fit any budget. And our finance department can discuss installment plans with you if necessary. Oh, and we have a couple of special plans on sale this week—and of course you get a five percent discount for being a referral!"

Barbaros made a foul exhalation that was probably a sigh of relief. He nodded and directed his attention to the colorful brochure Carol produced.

———

The bell tinkled again, admitting, this time, a small and rather vague looking person, whose presence only drew a nod from Carol, who went right back to her customer. "Now, if you could provide the exact coordinates of your lair on this line…"

"Uh…"

"That's fine if you don't know them off the top of your head." She brightly produced a tablet. "We can help you locate it via satellite. Here, I'll show you."

The vague individual, after nodding to Carol, opened the half door at one end of the service counter and headed for the back room.

"There we go!"

"Sorry about that…"

"Oh don't worry about it. Most people don't know their latitude and longitude exactly, that's why we have this." She put the tablet back with a glossy smile. "We use coordinates because they're globally applicable and, after all, our clients don't typically register a mailing address with the local postal authorities. All set!" She picked up a desk phone and punched one button. "Eugene? Are you free now to talk to a client? Okay, thanks, be right over." She beamed at Barbaros. "Now we'll have Eugene go over financing options with you. This way, please."

The vague individual in the back room dropped a light roast pod into the Keurig and switched it on, then rummaged through a file drawer and pulled out a few forms. These were spread upon the coffee table, and the individual retrieved the coffee, flopped onto the sagging old couch, and scribbled a pen on the corner of the paper a few times before starting to fill out the reports.

At the back of the back room, the bathroom door opened and a semi-transparent humanoid entered. "Oh, Corey, you're here?"

The vague Corey glanced up. "Hey. Yeah."

"Just in?"

"Mm."

The semi-transparent humanoid leaned around to look through the door to the lobby. "Did Carol have a client? I thought I heard someone."

"Mm. Taking him to Eugene." This said, Carol herself returned without Barbaros. She tidied up the front desk a bit and brought some papers into the back room.

"Ah. Probably not one for me, then?" This was directed at Carol.

Without the overpowering beam of her customer service smile and voice, Carol answered, "Doubt it. Sorry." Her lipstick looked oddly detached from the rest of her face when she wasn't beaming.

A sigh. "Guess I'll head home, then. Report's there." He pointed to a stack of papers. However, being semi-transparent, this only produced a frown from Carol.

"Where?"

The semi-transparent humanoid rolled his eyes, which no one detected, and crossed to the files to pick up and wave his report before setting it down again. "Okay? See you next week."

"Got it, thanks." Carol rifled the papers. Four seconds later, she said, "Ah! Gary!"

"What?" the voice called from the lobby.

"You didn't *sign* it—again!"

A mumbled apology as Carol delivered the report, and Gary signed it across the front desk. Corey continued filling out forms. Carol returned briskly, muttering under her breath, "…would remember to sign if he wants to get *paid*."

"He does," Corey said, eyes still on reports. "He's just not all there."

Carol rolled her head and eyes toward him and gave him a look that was by no means vague. In the pause of silence,

Corey glanced up at her, blinked, and returned the look to her, though now with considerably less visible meaning attached. Then, with a second blink, it was back to his report by way of a sip of coffee.

Nothing more passed between them in the back room for some minutes. Then the front desk phone buzzed on the inter-office line, and Carol leaned out through the door and grabbed it. "Yes? Yes. Okay, I'll tell him."

She hung up and returned. "The client picked you. You have time for an interview now, right?"

Corey raised his head and blinked, vaguely. "I don't have an opening for…two weeks?"

"He's fine with waiting, I guess. Budget."

A sigh. "Can you not put me on sale for a while? I'm busy enough."

Carol gave him a smile—not her customer one, but a dagger-sharp one that made her lipstick look a bit like blood. "Even on sale, your profit margin is the best."

"Only because I don't need support," Corey mumbled vaguely. "You're over-using me. They're going to catch on."

"Work hard so they don't!" Carol chirped.

Corey left the half-finished report and drifted back to the lobby, then down the hall to the conference room. Eugene was just arriving with the client, who had only slightly more space around him in the hallway than toothpaste has in a tube. Corey gave a vague nod that might have been for both or either of them, held out his hand, and watched his entire forearm vanish into the searing grasp of the client's handshake. "Mr. Barbaros," Corey hummed, "so nice to meet you. I'm Corey, your agent. Please, this way."

Eugene handed over Barbaros' file and returned to his office, Barbaros sidle-squeezed himself through the door, and Corey gazed vacantly at the conference table and the empty chairs. The chairs waited breathlessly in the pause. Then Corey gestured toward a loveseat over by the wall. "Have a seat." Barbaros mostly fit into the loveseat, which only slightly crunched and cracked under him as if it had been made of cardboard. Corey drew up his chair and began flipping through the forms Eugene had handed him. "Before we go into the details, Mr. Barbaros, did you have any questions I can help you with so far?"

"Ummm…" Barbaros folded his massive hands nervously in his massive lap. "Well, Eugene set up a payment plan so I could afford this, but I, uh, got to admit I went with you because you were the cheapest."

Expressionlessly: "There's nothing whatsoever wrong with that, Mr. Barbaros. Any of our agents can handle your retirement. My price point is low because my expenses are minimal; it doesn't mean I'm any less effective at the job."

"Oh no, I uh, didn't mean that. I'm sure you'll be great. But I, uh, noticed that there's some extra paperwork that comes with signing you. Stuff the others don't have…"

"You mean the liability for cancellation form?"

"Yeah."

"All right, let's start there." Corey settled into a vaguely professional and friendly posture, though his face was too blank to give any of it the right effect. "The liability form is just a policy we have in place in which you agree that you will be penalized if you should ever come out of retirement. It's mainly to protect our business. You need to be absolutely certain you want to retire if you're going to sign with me."

"Why?" Then Barbaros hurried to add, eyes widening, "I mean, I am! I totally am sure. I want to retire. But I mean…just curious."

"Because of the method I use to secure your retirement," Corey responded. He flipped through the papers and plucked one out and extended it. "Let's get to that. Here's an outline of the plan. As you can see, we're scheduled for…Thursday, two weeks. On that day, you'll need to schedule a final death match with your nemesis. Your own lair is preferred, but if you have a better location we can discuss that during this interview."

"My lair's fine…" Barbaros murmured.

"Great. So the way it typically goes is that you initiate the death match, use whatever fighting techniques your nemesis is familiar with so that they know it's really you. Then at a prearranged point, we switch." Corey gestured blandly at himself. "I'm a shapeshifter, so I take your form and get killed by your nemesis. You put down..." He scanned another form. "...Captain Valiant. Ah."

Barbaros growled a little.

Corey summoned his own valor and moved on without comment. "Yes, ah, so at the proper time, when Captain Valiant will believe it, I—as you—give a little death speech. I have a short form for you to fill out so I can make sure to say the last words you would prefer your nemesis to hear from you. Then I dissolve into dust and drift away on the breeze."

Looking a little slack-jawed, Barbaros blinked at him. "You do?"

"Mm. It's extremely effective at getting heroic specials to believe that you are really dead. To a certain extent, you could say it's the only real guarantee. Which is why we need you to sign the liability form when you choose me. If you later decided to come out of retirement and resume villainy—whether on a small scale or a global one—it would undermine the entire 'turn to dust' death. Heroic specials would eventually stop trusting it when they see someone turn to dust, and then I'd be out of a job." Corey shrugged in a way that was meant to be genial, but was too vague to be convincing.

"I can see how that would be a problem for you," Barbaros growled sympathetically. "That's definitely not an issue, though. I am totally serious about retirement. World domination has been a terrible hassle, not nearly as easy as I expected. It took me all year just to conquer Uganda, never mind the whole world." He rubbed his leathery brow with one hand, carefully not gouging his own eyes with his curved claws. "And with the way heroes are cropping up all over the place these days..."

Corey nodded. "Of course. Then here's the waiver to sign stating that you won't resume villainous pursuits—or," he tapped the paper in a certain spot, "reveal to anyone heroic that you are still alive. It's very important that your nemesis believes you genuinely dead, or your retirement will never be secure."

A vigorous nod. "Trust me. I bought a private island in Vanuatu. I'm going to disappear." He leaned back, to the loveseat's dismay. "Just soak up the sun and forget *Captain Valiant*." His voice snarled more than usual.

Without comment, Corey proceeded through the paperwork in a clear and concise manner.

———

With all final signatures secured, Corey returned and submitted the file to Carol, who was again all smiles and sweetness as Barbaros departed. Corey returned to finish his report, found his coffee cold, sighed, dumped it down the sink, and brewed another. Carol busily clicked and typed into the scheduling system, leafing through paperwork. She called back through the open door, "Sorry about your travel arrangements!"

Corey paused, pen hovering, blinked, and looked up at the door. After a vaguely pregnant pause, he asked, "Sorry." It didn't sound much like an asking.

"Well, his lair is in Uganda. It's a bit out of the way. And your schedule is a little tight."

"Whose fault is that," Corey mumbled.

"Tara is headed to Bhutan that same day, and Bingo has to be in Tokyo the day after, so I'm putting you on the jet with them. But they don't have time to take you all the way to Uganda, so I'm having the jet drop you in Doha and you can get a direct flight from there to Entebbe."

"So you're flying me commercial again."

"Only for part of it. Small part. Five hours forty."

Corey contemplated the opposite wall, gazing vaguely into the abyss of nearly six hours in a cramped economy-class seat. He could make himself smaller, of course, and he certainly would. That wasn't the point.

Leaning around the doorframe, Carol gave him a sparkling ruby smile. "I'll make it up to you. How about a long weekend? We won't schedule anything for that Friday, so after you're done with Barbaros you can take it easy for three days."

She took his vague blink as answer enough and whipped back around to her computer.

Corey returned to his abyss-gazing.

If he was on holiday, that meant the company's private jet wouldn't be dispatched to pick him up. He'd have to fly commercial all the way home. Corey estimated, based on experience, that between flight time and layovers, he wouldn't get home before Sunday morning—*if* everything went perfectly and there were no delays or cancellations.

The company would save a tidy little twenty grand. Corey would be in airports most of the weekend, if not all of it. And he was supposed to say "thank you" for the favor.

All this on top of letting Captain Valiant beat him "to death" *again*.

Corey signed his report with sharp precision and slapped it down on top of the intake pile for Carol.

2

At Entebbe International Airport, six armed guards were waiting for him, one of them awkwardly holding a sign with his name on it in front of the rifle he carried—and still kept in his hands. Corey drifted over to the guard and held out his phone; the guard proffered his own device, and Corey scanned the QR code and verified the identity of his escort. Then he followed them out of the rather dumpy little airport to the armored vehicle.

The weather was a beautiful, balmy 75 degrees, with a gentle breeze that helped to clear the stale stink of commercial flight out of Corey's lungs. The six guards were all identically dressed, identically silent, and fairly close to identical in appearance, too. In short, they were typical henchmen for a villain. Corey shut his eyes, and the drive passed in a vague silence.

The lair itself was a massive monstrosity situated on picturesque Lake Victoria. A shriveled minion ushered him into a room with large windows overlooking waters reflecting a clear blue sky. The room was an open concept with a lofted ceiling, and the color scheme was overwhelmingly black, with red used as an accent. The walls were hung with hideous blades of mysterious variety, and the décor was suggestive of an eclectic taxidermist. Barbaros offered him a seat on something vaguely chair-shaped that looked like it would have probably attempted to eat Corey, had it still been able to do so. He sat down, vaguely consoled to think that the furniture no longer had a stomach. It did, however, still possess all its teeth.

"Tea?"

Corey glanced at the proffered cup that looked like some sort of unholy grail, filled with a gently steaming Ceylon. "Thanks." He accepted the drink. He sipped. "Nice place," he said.

Barbaros made one of his hideous snarling expressions that didn't much resemble a wince, but tried to. "Uh, thanks. I hired an interior decorator."

"Did you?" Corey asked, blandly. He glanced around. He did not raise his eyebrows to any significant degree.

Barbaros coughed. "Yeah. She, uh, sort of chose her design theme based on my name and went from there." He paused. Then he added, "It's roomy."

"That's certainly an advantage," Corey acknowledged.

Some tea-sipping passed between them.

"Good flight?"

Corey hummed vaguely.

"You flew in from Qatar, right?"

Corey hummed a vague affirmative.

"That's good. I've done that a few times myself. It's not too bad."

Corey hummed his vaguest hum of all.

"When I first came here, though, that was a horrible flight. I flew in from Heathrow, we were delayed on the tarmac for over an hour, there was turbulence…" Barbaros growled in a most dissatisfied way at the recollection.

The primary source of Corey's curiosity upon hearing this was: *how did he fit on a commercial jet?* Since that would have been a rude question to ask his client, Corey said, "When you first came here? Aren't you from here?"

Barbaros gave him a demonically startled expression. "No? I'm Canadian."

"Ah." A pause. "If I may ask, why did you choose to take over Uganda? Canada would probably have given you less trouble."

Barbaros looked monstrously uncomfortable. "Well, some things happened and…I left. I—I wouldn't attempt it. My, uh, sister is still there."

"Your sister." Corey's polite expression of inquiry was too vague to make out. "Is she also a special?"

"Huh? No, she's normal. Totally normal."

"Mmm."

Corey decided that "Where are you from?" had played itself out as a polite inquiry and was heading into personal territory, so he spent some time sipping his tea instead.

"When is your nemesis arriving?"

"Oh. Uh, not until dark, I think."

Corey nodded vaguely. Really, it had been a painfully thin attempt at a topic. Obviously, Captain Valiant wouldn't fight his nemesis at two in the afternoon on a beautiful 75-degree day. If it wasn't raining heavily, the death match would simply have to wait for dark, or at least sunset.

Unfortunately, Corey couldn't really discuss the retirement plan with his client. The paperwork was quite thorough, and there was little left to discuss. Corey asked to use the lavatory, and after doing that and finishing his tea, Barbaros suggested a tour of the lair so that they could arrange the location for swapping places during the death match.

That being the goal, Corey felt the tour ended up being a little excessively thorough.

"Of course, I can't put carpet in here. It's just impossible, with the way the whole dungeon floods twice a year. The contractor didn't install the drains properly. It's a constant struggle to keep the damp out, even when it's not the rainy season. In spring, this whole level is just a lake." He shook his massive head hopelessly.

Corey glanced around. Each cell had a dehumidifier running in it. "Theoretically, this is where you keep your enemies, though?"

"Well, yeah." Barbaros blinked red eyes at him. "I torture those who oppose me, but it's not like I would expose them to *mold*. Biotoxin illness is serious."

"Ah." Corey nodded vaguely.

Barbaros spent almost twenty minutes discussing the drains—what was wrong with them, and why they didn't work—before he concluded their tour of the empty dungeon.

———

The death match occurred during a truly beautiful African sunset. Barbaros was initially worried that the swap would be difficult to pull off. However, Corey had previous files on Captain Valiant and could reassure Barbaros that the heroic special's x-ray vision was blocked by polyurethane. The walls of Barbaros' evil lair were insulated with polyurethane foam insulation, among many, many other things, so all they needed to do was get a wall between Barbaros and his nemesis for a moment and Corey could smoothly take over.

There was just one problem. Captain Valiant brought a sidekick.

For a moment, Corey was afraid the sidekick would derail their entire plan by flanking Barbaros and making it hard to get entirely out of sight, even for a brief moment. However, it turned out that she was either a trainee or just one of those bits of arm candy heroic specials sometimes acquired, because she hung back and didn't get close enough to the fight to present a problem.

Then it was all on Corey to do his job.

He found the form of Barbaros a little inconvenient. He felt heavy, and the spikes and chains of his apparel were extremely inconvenient. It was a good thing he didn't have to actually fight while dressed like this; his part was mainly to let Captain Valiant beat him up a bit more, and to appear more heavily injured than he really was. And, of course, he had a line to deliver.

Corey lay on the top of the highest turret, bleeding and gasping, as Captain Valiant flew up and faced him in the last light of the dying sun. Corey glared virulent hatred at him and, between heavy, labored breaths, delivered his line:

"Curse you…the world…shall be mine…you *twerp*."

————

To backtrack slightly, four hours before this:

"And you put here that you want your final words to be…" Corey scanned the form. "Ah, 'Curse you the world shall be mine'?" He glanced up at Barbaros. "Is that all?"

Barbaros twiddled his colossal thumbs. "Yeah. Why?"

"It's a bit impersonal?" Corey said. *Cliché*, he didn't say.

A shrug. "I don't know. He's not really my nemesis for personal reasons. He's just the first heroic brat who stuck his nose in my business and decided it was his job to stop me taking over any more countries. He's annoying, and I'm sick of dealing with him, but I'm just as sick of dealing with ruling the world. Or, you know, Uganda."

In a thoroughly vague murmur, Corey said, "He does have a habit of doing that."

————

"You what?"

But Corey said no more. Captain Valiant watched, slightly taken aback, as Corey performed his signature shift and dissolved into dust and drifted away on the breeze. He reconstituted himself as a pebble just out of sight and settled himself to wait until the heroic and his sidekick were gone.

"Huh."

The girl ran up behind him. "Valley! Are you okay?"

"I'm fine. Let's go, he's dead."

"Are you sure?"

"Totally. Didn't you see him turn into dust?"

"So?"

"That means they're completely dead and can't come back. How about dinner?"

"Why does turning into dust mean that?"

"What do you mean?"

14

"Well, I mean, we're specials, but we do still have physical bodies with like, pretty normal biology. And you just punched him a lot. It's not like he got hit by lightning or fell into some kind of radiation field. Why would a body just spontaneously dissolve into dust? Sure, after being dead for a few years. Or you know, if you get cremated, absolutely. But this guy was just here, getting punched, and now he's vanished. Doesn't that seem weird?"

Corey the tiny pebble felt cold dread wash over his rocky surface and settle in a pit in the center of his...center. *A smart one.*

Captain Valiant had been gazing around in an abstracted manner. When his sidekick stopped talking, he snapped back to her with a bright smile. "Absolutely. Dinner's on me."

The girl gave him a confused look and said, "I wanna look around a bit before we leave."

Smart, cautious, and thorough, Corey amended.

"Great! We can do that."

Corey waited as Captain Valiant wandered off in a mild oblivion. The sidekick began a careful search of the area and soon descended to the far side of the evil lair, out of sight. Barbaros was well concealed, if he had followed the plan; Corey wasn't worried about that. But he had vague misgivings about this girl and her ideas. She wouldn't find anything—this time. But he couldn't have her putting her revolutionary notions into Captain Valiant's spacious head.

It pained him—oh how it pained him!—to do this, but he had no choice. Drawing upon all his fortitude, Corey shifted into the all-too-familiar shape of Captain Valiant.

Back on two legs, Corey stood a moment, not-his skin crawling. Then, with a deep breath, he carefully did *not* look down at himself, but quickly followed the trail the departing sidekick had taken.

He located her on the far side of the lair, in the last light of sunset and the gathering softness of twilight. It was at this point that Corey noticed that this sidekick was a little unusual for a special: she wasn't built like an hourglass that got a little too excited about its own shape. She didn't have a face like every plastic surgeon's "after" posters. She was mainly just…normal. Kind of cute, if anything. Probably why she was only a sidekick. She didn't have the supermodel features required for a champion of justice.

She was still scouring the area, but she glanced at him briefly as he approached. "Oh, Valley. Find anything?"

Corey faintly cleared not-his throat. "Nothing," he said. Then: "You see, what happens is that, ah, all specials are born with elevated levels of electromagnetic…fields. You know, every life form has its own bioelectric signature, and specials are enhanced. The use of their powers increases the interaction between matter and energy in their bodies. So when a special follows a heroic or villainous profession, which requires them to use their powers regularly, the bioelectric energy field permeates their cellular matrixes to such an extent that the sudden extinguishing of this field causes a catastrophic failure of structural integrity. In short, they break up. Disintegrate. That's what you saw happen. So you see, Barbaros is really dead. We can leave."

Thank you, Star Trek, Corey thought.

The girl blinked at him, her mouth open slightly. "Valley?"

"What?"

"What's with all the long words?"

A creeping wave of vagueness began to steal over him. Corey snapped it off with a bright Captain Valiant grin. "Anyway, dinner? Dinner, right? I'll just be at the…" He pointed behind himself, but suddenly realized he hadn't paid attention to what kind of vehicle the heroics had arrived in. *Plane? Car? Helicopter?* He backed away. "I'll just. You know. Whenever you finish up here."

The moment he rounded the corner, Corey returned to the refuge of being a pebble. A moment later, the sidekick rounded the corner after him, saying, "Valley, what the— oh." Captain Valiant was nowhere in sight. She sighed. "He didn't have to use super speed. What is wrong with him today." She huffed, glanced around one last time, and muttered, "Structural disintegration?" Then she left.

Corey remained as a deeply relieved pebble for the next five minutes. When he was certain he was now safe from both the twerp and his cute sidekick, he returned to his usual vague form and went to rendezvous with his client and wrap things up.

He had at least 30 hours of travel ahead.

———— ———— ————

As it turned out, Corey was forced to accept his client's hospitality for the night. There were no late flights leaving Entebbe; he had to wait to catch the first flight out Friday morning. Fortunately, Barbaros was extremely civil about the whole thing. Unfortunately, the guest bedrooms in the lair were consistent with the rest of the décor theme, but there wasn't much Barbaros could do about that at this point. His goons escorted Corey back to the airport first thing in the morning. Then Corey had an eight-hour layover in Dubai; his connection to Heathrow was changed to Rome; he was stuck in Rome for six hours waiting for a connection to New York; when it came time to board, *that* plane was delayed for two hours and eventually cancelled due to a repair issue; he was scheduled back onto a flight to Heathrow; he had another four-hour layover once he got there; and finally, Sunday afternoon, he landed in Chicago. When he took his phone out of airplane mode, he had a message waiting from Carol. She wanted to see him at the company extra early Monday morning for a client interview before they sent him off on his next scheduled job.

3

Carol thought Corey was looking vaguely murderous when he showed up Monday morning. She had observed before that he had a way of darkening in color when his general outlook was less than chipper. Therefore, whereas some poor simpletons might have smiled at Corey and remarked that he looked like he got a nice tan in Africa, Carol buttoned it and employed professional detachment. She handed him the file for his interview and didn't say anything about it when she saw him taking his coffee with him to the conference room—technically against policy.

Corey's paperwork was finished in record time, sharp and crisp in every detail. One of Carol's penciled eyebrows twitched upward; beyond that, she did not comment. "I have you on the jet for São Paolo with Lucy—she's going to Cape Town. It leaves at four this afternoon." She watched Corey give no indication of any reaction to this. His blank stare gave her the courage to explain: "You should be able to sleep on the jet, and you land about 7 a.m. And it's only two hours' time difference. You can get a little unscrambled."

"The jet," Corey said. And that was all he said.

"Yes!" Carol cut up diamonds with the edges of her smile.

"For just me and Lucy."

"Your client this time is an exceptionally high-paying one. I'm not even sure why Diabola picked you. She could afford any agent. She's already conquered most of South America, according to reports."

Still flat, Corey answered: "In the interview, if I remember, she particularly wanted the plan I provide."

"Well, who can blame her," Carol chirped. "I suppose we all want to evaporate into dust now and again. Have a nice trip!"

Corey did. He had an unusually nice trip. The company jet was partially fitted out like a luxury hotel room inside. Corey was unconscious before liftoff and remained so until it was time to disembark.

———

It was already a warmish day in São Paolo when Corey hit fresh air at 7:34 a.m., following his escort. Diabola had not sent armed guards; her secretary picked Corey up and rode in the back of the limo with him as the chauffeur took them to Diabola's lair.

Diabola's lair was a magnificent luxury estate built into a cliff overlooking a clear, sparkling sea. Whether she had hired an interior decorator or not, there was nothing overtly "devilish" in her décor theme. Polished marble and granite, natural wood, bamboo—this particular evil lair was built on the model of a vacationer's tropical paradise.

The secretary presented Corey to his client poolside. Diabola was a stunning Latina in a strappy swimsuit, but Corey was rather inured to that sort of thing. Specials tended toward extreme good looks or else some sort of monstrous disfiguration. There was a pronounced correlation between good looks and heroic professions, as well as disfiguration with villainy, but the ranks of the villainous were not without their occasional drop-dead gorgeous evil temptress. The ranks of the heroics similarly contained a few who weren't qualified for a supermodel, but in that case, they tended to be sidekicks. And even sidekicks, Corey mused, were at least…cute.

Diabola fell into the evil temptress class; so be it. It hardly mattered. Dark lords of all varieties were unlikely to tempt their retirement agents.

Diabola glanced at him through the latest luxury sunglasses and smiled, waving toward an extremely comfortable outdoor sofa. "You are punctual," she said. The sharply dressed fellow standing behind the outdoor bar came forward and asked Corey if he could get him anything. Corey requested soda water with key lime and got it. He watched the bartender step over to the edge of a sprawling garden and pick the key limes for him off a tree. "Locally sourced," Diabola purred, "whenever possible. And of course, entirely organic and non-GMO."

"Delicious," Corey agreed, vaguely. And it was.

"I fear the moron will be arriving for a lunch date," Diabola continued, tone airily apologetic as she got straight to business. "That will not be a problem, I hope? Is your dust…" She waved a hand delicately, long and glossy nails catching the sun, "…*thing* more difficult in full sun? If need, we can use the deep shade in the garden. Only if we really must. I hate to put danger to the plants."

"I can assure you that time of day has no effect on your retirement plan. It's only customary. Heroic specials seem to expect either darkness or poor weather conditions when they face their nemeses."

Diabola laughed dismissively and did not take up the topic of Captain Valiant. "Well, I look forward to your work. If you retire Diabola flawlessly, I will be pleased to use your services again in future."

Corey frowned vaguely and felt moderately piqued. "May I remind you of the additional liability form you signed when—"

But Diabola's glossy fingernails were flashing sunlight in his eyes again as she waved this away. "Oh, Diabola will retire, do not worry. But I am not really Diabola." She paid no attention to Corey or his vaguely questioning look. "I am

Meta Morpha." She tossed her luxurious dark hair regally. "I shall rise with a new name and face, and I shall conquer a new part of the world. And I shall do it again and again, as often as I like, and no one will know my true face." She smiled at Corey now. "You see, we are not so different, you and I."

Corey blinked at her once. He considered this, and decided that his client wasn't in breach of contract. Then he observed somewhat dryly, "Aren't you generally expected to say that to your nemesis?"

Full, dark lips curled in distaste. "That moron? Why would I insult myself? He and I are *entirely* different."

Corey re-attended to his drink. "At present," he mumbled. Then, clearer: "If you have shapeshifting abilities, why did you decide to hire a retirement agency?"

"Ah." Diabola shrugged her slim, sculpted shoulders. "It is a little different. The cocoon, the chrysalis, the butterfly, you see?" She smiled, flicking her flashy fingernails again. "It takes a little time. And I cannot be dust." The disparaging tone she said this in made Corey a little unclear on whether her abilities were limited in such a way that dust was impossible for her, or whether she simply disdained the form. "The dust is important, I understand. The moron believes in it?"

A short nod. "Thus far, to the best of our knowledge, all the heroics interpret a person dissolving into dust as the definitive indicator of permanent death." *Except possibly…* But Corey withheld that comment.

"Excellent. Now to the rest of the arrangements."

In preparing for the final battle, Corey and Diabola hit a rather serious snag. Diabola's lair was built of one hundred percent all-natural materials. Polyurethane was nowhere in evidence. Even the ubiquitous foam insulation was absent; cold was not a major concern in São Paolo.

"Well, at least there's Spandex, though it can be awkward to set up…"

"There is no Spandex," Diabola interrupted, with considerable disdain. This froze Corey in vague disbelief for a moment. He blinked mildly at his client. "All of my clothing is made with natural fibers," she added haughtily. "This is pure Sea Island cotton."

Corey lowered his gaze by a few degrees. Somewhat unprofessionally, perhaps, he simply asked, "How do you get cotton to fit like *that?*" Diabola had changed from her swimsuit into a high-fashion villainess outfit that Corey would have described as "typical" or, if pressed, "snug."

"Tailoring." She shrugged.

Corey cleared his throat and blandly resumed his professionalism. "Are you saying there is nothing synthetic in your lair?"

"I cannot say," Diabola hummed. Then she summoned her secretary and put the question to him.

The secretary gave the question some thought and finally said, "Your mattress is memory foam, my lady."

"Ah!" Diabola's eyes widened in realization. "Yes, I was forced to make that exception." She gave Corey a grave look. "Proper sleep is extremely important."

Corey's answer was delayed a moment; when it came, it was entirely flat: "No, of course. Wouldn't dream of missing it."

So they planned it:

Since the mattress was the only polyurethane in the lair and Captain Valiant was coming for lunch and they didn't have time to remodel, Corey would need to hide under Diabola's bed for the swap.

Since Diabola didn't want to risk any battle damage to the interior of her house *or*, of course, her garden, the bed would be moved outside. Six goons were summoned by the secretary to lug the bed out to the pool deck—then six more were summoned, because memory foam is really heavy. Diabola insisted on changing the bedspread and camouflaging it to look a little more like it was designed to be outdoor furniture. Corey didn't argue with his client; he had to agree that the bed looked less suspiciously out of place once it was draped with a sea foam linen spread instead of the dark evergreen comforter.

Then Diabola had to change into her battle gear, and Corey had to change into Diabola in her battle gear and hide under her bed and wait his timing.

Finally, they were ready.

Then Captain Valiant showed up with his sidekick and nearly ruined everything:

"Haha, villain! You don't stand a chance against me! NitroGirl, you deal with her."

Corey frowned, hearing this, and scooted closer to the edge of the bed, listening.

"But Valley—I mean, Captain—um, she conquered almost a whole continent and I'm just a side—"

"Don't be silly. She's a woman; I can't beat up a woman. You fight her."

Crap.

Diabola's voice had lost its usual deep smoothness. "You must be joking to me."

NitroGirl attacked, and Diabola threw off the attack impatiently. Corey's mind raced. After a few more unsuccessful attempts by the sidekick, Diabola managed to pretend to be pushed back toward the bed. There, she put up an energy cocoon for defense, then muttered over her shoulder to Corey, "It seems I remember some little thing in the contracts that says I cannot kill the heroics while using your services."

"You definitely can't. There are major penalties for actually killing a heroic, and you'd be blacklisted from ever using my company's services again."

"I see. Well then. How do I pretend to be beaten anywhere near to death by this little thing?"

Still hidden under the bed, Corey tried to keep the tension out of his voice. "The only thing you can do is knock her out."

"How can I, without killing her?"

Corey didn't argue the point. He guessed that Diabola knew her own strength. "What about restraining her? Do you have any abilities that would put her under restraint that she can't escape from?"

"Oh, many," she agreed, "but they will kill her too."

"Immediately?"

"Well, quickly."

"What's the slowest?"

"Mm. I can trap her in a web. Usually it takes about ten minutes to kill a heroic, but her—only five, no more."

Corey winced. "Then do it and tell Captain Valiant that it'll only take one minute. We'll have to rush your death a bit."

Diabola sighed annoyance, muttered, "Tacky," and dropped the cocoon. Corey heard a girl's voice yelp a moment later, and then Diabola was making her threat to Captain Valiant.

"Becky! Noooooooo!" Corey almost—*almost*—leaned a tiny bit out from under the bed. *Her name is Becky?* Then: "You monster!" And, from the sound of it, Captain Valiant was finally fighting his latest nemesis.

Things got back on track from there, and in short order Diabola was able to roll under the bed. Corey had literally half a second to observe and duplicate her injuries and put himself into his own roll, leaving by the opposite side. Then Diabola worked on releasing the sidekick from her spell while Corey worked on pretending to get killed. And, of course, he had to deliver Diabola's last words, as listed on the paperwork.

Corey generally didn't care much about the size or shape of the body he was in. For him, becoming a busty, gorgeous Latina was really no different than becoming a hulking monster. But shapeshifting aside, Corey wasn't a fantastic actor. He could usually manage the villain's last words, but he was glad his job didn't go too far beyond that.

Diabola was overworking him, a bit—but then, she was an extremely high-paying client.

Corey was pinned to the earth by Captain Valiant's sword, but he made his voice as smooth and seductive as he could. With a flirtatious half-smile, he raised a bloody hand and drew one long, perfectly manicured fingernail along Captain Valiant's ridiculously square jaw. "Let's meet again in

Mumbai, darling," he purred, and then sighed—with feigned weakness and real relief—as he dissolved into dust.

Diabola, now hiding under her own bed, finished releasing the spell holding NitroGirl. Corey reconstituted himself as a tree frog in the nearby garden and rolled his froggy eyes over to see if the sidekick was all right. It had been a potentially deadly web, after all.

There was the sound of nonspecific coughing, and then: "Valley!"

"Becky! Are you all right?"

Coughing: "I'll be fine…did you beat her?"

"She's gone, babe, don't worry about it."

Babe. Corey the tree frog licked his eyeball. This, it turns out, is how tree frogs express themselves during moments of profound chagrin.

"I told you I couldn't handle a villain that strong yet…"

There was some noodley mush following this. Corey listened with stoic courage, enduring the nonsense in order to make certain that the heroics expressed no doubts about his dissolve-to-dust death. On this occasion, however, the clever sidekick was a little occupied with her own near-death, and was willing to take Captain Valiant's word for it that everything was over. Captain Valiant, of course, had stopped thinking about Diabola the moment "she" turned to dust. Out of sight was, in his case, quite literally out of mind.

At last, the heroics departed, Corey returned to his usual vague self, and Diabola emerged from hiding under her bed with a regal grace so pointedly excessive that it was threatening.

Corey was mild and diplomatic and kept things on a business level. "I'm not certain he understood or will remember your hint about India, but I hope my delivery was satisfactory."

Diabola was painstakingly fixing her askew spikes. "Satisfactory, yes." Her posture remained incredible. Such poise could never be managed by anyone who had ever in their lives even thought about hiding under a bed. "The entire day has not been, I admit, quite as I imagined, but some part is due to my own lack of preparation. If the idiot does annoy my next form, I will bear in mind the matter of the synthetic material. If some other miserable hero tries me, I will make certain we communicate much in advance, so that we are prepared better than today."

"I'll put a special note in your file," Corey agreed, "and if you would like, I can set up a QR code for you before I go, and you can be your own referral for next time."

Diabola nodded, seeming mollified. Even a villainess who owned almost an entire continent appreciated five percent off.

4

When Corey drifted into the office, Carol was painting her fingernails. She glanced at him. "Toby's here," was all she said, and Corey nodded vaguely.

"Noted."

He went to the back room to pick up the forms he needed to fill out.

The back room was rather full.

There was a Toby by the Keurig, poking at his mug as it filled. There was a Toby rummaging through the file drawer, muttering form numbers. There was a Toby lying on the couch staring at the ceiling with his mouth open. By the sound of water running, there was a Toby in the bathroom. As Corey hesitated, a Toby came in, apparently from a client interview. He promptly split into two Tobies, one taking one part of his file with him to the couch, the other taking the rest of his file to the filing cabinet and joining up with that Toby.

Corey swept the room with an expressionless gaze. "Are you done with anything yet?"

The Toby at the Keurig glanced at him, picking up his mug. "Done with this," he said.

"Thanks." Corey went over and began preparing his own light roast, while the coffee-carrying Toby went to the couch Toby and set down the coffee. As he sat down, the reclining Toby sat up, and they became one Toby.

Corey focused on his coffee, ignoring the Toby who came out of the bathroom and joined with the filing cabinet Toby. When that one was done and the filing cabinet was free, Corey took his opportunity to get his own paperwork together. The room was getting a little less crowded as several Tobies became one Toby. Corey hoped there would soon be room for him to sit down and fill out his forms.

However, filing cabinet Toby dropped the paperwork on the coffee table and then meandered off again; the sitting Toby picked up a pen and his coffee in his right hands, and then one of him got up and also walked off. The wandering Tobies didn't seem to be engaged in much, but they were getting in Corey's way in the small back room.

"Toby?"

"Mm?" All of them looked at him.

"Could you join up for a while? You're in the way."

"Oh, sure," all of them said.

The meandering Tobies joined the Toby on the couch who was doing paperwork. As soon as there was only one of him, Toby suddenly blinked at Corey. "Oh, hey, back from South America?"

"You knew I was in South America?"

"One of me must have heard it somewhere."

"Huh."

"Oh, here, have a seat." The one and only remaining Toby scooted over to make room for Corey to sit and do his own paperwork.

"Thanks."

They filled out their reports on their latest clients in silence.

Toby finished first, and he was considerate enough to all stand up together to file his report. "I'm on a two-week vacation starting next week, so if none of me sees ya, good luck on your next jobs."

"Thanks. Where are you going on vacation?"

"Alaska, Bahamas, Venice, Bangkok, and this temple in Nepal where you can do a two-week retreat and live with the monks."

"Sounds nice," Corey said, vaguely, though to him it sounded like a bit much, even for several people.

"I'm all excited," Toby agreed, then waved and departed.

Carol came in, picked up his report, and promptly slapped it back down on the intake tray. "I'm going to *kill* one of him."

"Did he write every word five times again?"

"*Every. Single. Word.*"

Corey shrugged vaguely. "What do you expect? He's a scatterbrain."

————

For over a month, Corey did not have to get "killed" by Captain Valiant. He had a variety of other heroic specials to fool, and his schedule was packed. Carol had him do quite a few of his initial client interviews via Zoom call. The clients couldn't wait around until he was back in the country.

In fact, Corey was booked so tight that Carol began stringing his clients together. He made it back to the office about once a week; he submitted his reports electronically; and though he sometimes got picked up by the company jet for a few of his connections, the majority of his travel was commercial. Carol flashed him a slicing red smile and told him she had worked *extra hard* to arrange all his destinations in one general direction. He circled the globe approximately weekly, usually going east and cropping each of his days a little shorter; once, he reversed and went west, and all his days ran on too long. Carol argued strongly in favor of this approach, claiming that it was much less jet lag because he only had to adjust to a few hours' change per day and he wasn't hopping back and forth.

Corey made a rather pointed comment about most people needing more than a single day to adjust to a five-hour time difference, and he made the observation with a kind of sharp clarity that shut Carol up. So she worked harder to sell a few of the other agents instead of Corey, whenever possible, in an effort to free him up for some vacation time. She even bumped Corey's rate up a little bit, because he was such a hot commodity among the semi-successful, lower-middle-class range of villains. She put Lucy and Gary on sale, for three days only, just so that there would be a couple agents who were cheaper than Corey for a little bit.

Unfortunately, there was only so much Carol could do. Money was money. Carol had sworn she would get Corey home for a break—she even wrote herself a sticky note and put it right in the center top of the frame of her computer monitor—but then Countess Cryo just *had* to have the "dissolve to dust" agent that Diabola had retired with. And when Carol tried to tell her that Corey wasn't available, the temperature in the office plummeted to twenty bellow, and it wasn't about to stop there.

Carol gave in and booked Corey for another job, thus rescuing her fingers from frostbite so that they might live to clackity-clack on her keyboard for another day.

———

The agent in the field knew none of this. What Corey knew what that he was tired. What Corey knew was that every flight had at least one screaming baby on it. What Corey knew was that jet lag didn't work the way Carol thought it did. What Corey knew was that Super Trooper had very nearly managed to actually hurt him when Corey was pretending to get killed, and CaliguLava had been rude about it and not concerned at all.

What Corey knew was that he hadn't seen Captain Valiant in a month—more, actually. Two days short of six weeks, as a matter of fact. And he didn't want to. He was glad. He didn't like Captain Valiant. He didn't know how anyone *could*. In fact, anyone who liked that boulder-jawed, pudding-brained, empty-eyed carboard cutout of a bodybuilder was just plain *stupid*.

Then his nonstop redeye fight from Tokyo back to the states was cancelled by a message from Carol—and one more job before he could go home. At least she had the company jet pick him up and drop him off in Hawai'i.

Small mercies, he thought, because the downside was right there in black and white on the paperwork.

Nemesis: *Captain Valiant.*

5

Thanks to the company jet, Corey was able to bypass Honolulu and land directly in Kona, on the Big Island, rather than having to get a puddle-jumper from Oahu. The weather in Kona was a sunny, breezy 80 degrees when Corey landed. The slopes of Hualālai loomed in the distance, black with volcanic basalt.

Countess Cryo sent a goon to pick him up in a commandeered tour bus.

There were villains and then there were villains, after all. Some villains, through a series of unfortunate events known only to themselves, ended up in destabilized regions and took advantage of the chaos. Some villains were clever and staggeringly successful and wealthy and decided to retire because they knew the odds of survival for a heroic special's nemesis. Some villains could barely afford to retire; some retired in style. Occasionally, they even retired due to reaching a normal human retirement age and deciding that they were tired of maiming and terrorizing and would quite fancy a bit of golf for a change.

And some villains just lived rich in vacation destinations and had inherited a whole lot of money from their daddies and set up as a local tyrant because it was stylish, or to make connections, or because they were bored. And perhaps they retired because a particularly fashionable villainess had set the trend, or because they wanted to enter politics, or because they were bored.

It wasn't Corey's job to wonder about the reasons for the fabulous ice palace on top of Hualālai. It was his job to dissolve into dust so that Captain Valiant would dismiss Countess Cryo from his mind and she could go do whatever it was she planned to do next—which was also none of Corey's business.

The bus was not equipped with a heater, because it was a Hawai'ian tour bus. As they neared the lair, the temperature steadily fell, landing at about 45 degrees when Corey got out of the bus. He had already opened his suitcase during the ride and pulled out a fleece jacket. He had been in Oslo earlier that week.

The lair was about the size of a football stadium, and it was stunningly beautiful, but from the look of it, the whole thing was, in fact, made of ice. The interior was probably not what you might call "balmy," Corey mused vaguely.

Countess Cryo posed in the massive, grand entrance, a towering ice staff in one hand. She appeared to be channeling Maleficent by way of Gucci, after a few years locked in a walk-in freezer. Corey had a vague impression that he remembered seeing that particular fashion monstrosity of a dress a few years ago, being worn by a particularly successful villainous temptress. But of course, his memory, like his expression, could often be fuzzy on these things.

Countess Cryo herself was at that special stage of life when it was time to stop trying to look 25, time to tone down the colors in her makeup, and *definitely* time to raise the neckline on her dresses a little bit. Judging by the present evidence before him, Corey would surmise that Countess Cryo disagreed about her own time of life and took a different view. Perhaps she thought it was still working for her. Regardless, she was regal in the extreme and left quite an impression.

Her retirement agent, who left no impression whatsoever, approached her, files and paperwork already in hand, and opened the meeting with, "Countess Cryo, a pleasure. There are a few additional forms I need to go over with you at your earliest convenience."

In answer, the Countess released a peal of cackling laughter that could have been recorded and kept as a stock sound effect to use in any movie involving a witch. Then, suddenly cutting herself off mid-cackle, she intoned, "We shall speak over dinner, which is to be al fresco. Some of the dishes are meant to be taken warm."

Behind the ice palace was a non-ice pavilion poised on the edge of the volcano's crater. The goon served them takeout from a local restaurant. Perhaps this was the price you paid for an ice palace—it made cooking difficult.

"First of all," Corey began, without preamble, "just to confirm, you have been informed of the polyurethane requirement with Captain Valiant?"

Countess Cryo unleashed her pealing witch cackle again—quite without warning. Her fork hovered halfway to her mouth while she cackled, and the pasta upon her fork waited patiently to be eaten. When she ceased laughing, it was as sudden as a light switching off. She said, "Yes." Then she completed the doom of her pasta.

There was an indistinct pause while Corey waited for further information and Countess Cryo chewed. However, when she had swallowed the lamented pasta, she did not speak to Corey again. Instead, her darkly-mascaraed eyes widened at her crystalline—but not actually ice, for obvious reasons—plate, and she said, "You look *just like* that miserable meathead hero." And she stabbed viciously at another helpless penne.

Thinking that perhaps the upshot of his initial question had gone a bit sideways, Corey made a vague sound that was meant for throat-clearing. "May I ask what sort of polyurethane-containing materials you have around here? We'll need to plan how we may use it for cover."

Ice-clear eyes blinked at him. "This pavilion is plastic. I ordered it special from Home Depot."

Corey nodded. He had been wondering about this pavilion. The plastic composites mimicked real wood and stone, and the whole thing was huge and very fancy. But set up next to a magical ice palace that sparkled in the sun, the pavilion had a suspiciously suburban look. Not that Captain Valiant would notice a thing. But Corey wondered what his sidekick would think.

However, the more immediate issue was that the pavilion was a totally open structure that provided no cover whatsoever. Corey said so.

"Oh." Countess Cryo glanced around, mildly annoyed. "You cannot hide here?"

"I," Corey explained, "can hide under this spoon, if I need to. But *you* can't, and we need to keep you out of sight after I take your place, or else Captain Valiant will realize you aren't dead—when he sees you alive."

Countess Cryo reacted with a burst of cackling. However, Corey soon dismissed the idea that she was amused by anything he had said. He wasn't entirely sure she had heard what he said, actually. She appeared to be laughing at her salad.

"If I might make a suggestion," he continued, "we may still be able to use the pavilion—or at least the roof. Do you think that during your fight with Captain Valiant you could knock these support pillars down?"

Countess Cryo gazed at him for a minute, saying nothing.

It occurred to Corey that it might be occurring to Countess Cryo that plastic more or less stayed where it was if you froze it or covered it in ice. Corey didn't have a full listing of Countess Cryo's powers, but so far the only thing he had witnessed was an ability to make the area around her cold and to shape ice. Optional skills in eardrum-damaging laughter. "Or," he suggested, "you could also take cover behind the support pillars and let your nemesis knock them down for you."

A light of revelation dawned in Countess Cryo's eyes, but she remained aloof in tone. "That will be acceptable." Then, without preamble, she dumped the rest of her pasta bolognaise on her nearby goon's head. "Yes—blood, blood, *blood!* Let their blood rain from the skies!" The goon, as if expecting this, raised the parmesan grater and began to grind parmesan cheese onto his head.

Corey felt a slight concern that the lunch meeting was getting a bit off track, so he resumed the topic of the battle with Captain Valiant. "The next matter I need to discuss with you is a somewhat recent development our agency has encountered with your nemesis, Captain Valiant." Corey withdrew another form from his file folder and placed it on top of the stack of paperwork. "He has acquired a sidekick called NitroGirl. In a recent encounter with a female client," Corey kept the name out of it to protect his client's confidentiality, "Captain Valiant instructed his sidekick to fight. He seems to have developed a compunction—" Countess Cryo blinked at him. "—A sense of guilt about personally fighting a female nemesis. So it is possible that he will stand back and send NitroGirl to fight you instead."

"Oh?" Countess Cryo didn't seem to find anything in this worth comment.

"Which means," Corey clarified, "that you'll need to pretend to be beaten almost to death by his sidekick. Does this present any problems for you?"

"I am a fantastic actress!" Countess Cryo said at once. She followed this with another peal of cackling laughter.

Corey slightly opened his mouth, stopped, closed it, and gave a vague nod. "Do you want to provide an alternate set of 'last words' for the sidekick?" He held his pen poised above the form.

"What did I put for the stupid man?" Countess Cryo leaned forward a bit, frowning at the form. Corey compliantly turned it toward her and indicated the spot where he had typed in her answer during their Zoom call. "Ah." She shrugged. "The female counterpart to that word will do."

Corey jotted one five-letter word on the line for "Alternate Final Words." Countess Cryo began plucking up individual droplets of water from her water glass with her fingertip and dropping them into a little pile of ice beads on the table.

"All right, I think that's nearly everything. I just need to ask about your lair." He pointed. "Is it at all maintained by your special abilities?"

"Entirely." The Countess looked very proud of herself.

"In that case, I'll need you to cease maintaining it starting from the moment when I turn to dust. All evidence of your powers needs to vanish at that moment."

At this, Countess Cryo suddenly leapt to her feet, slamming her hand down on the table. Her pile of ice beads scattered with the cacophony of a sudden, tiny little hailstorm. "You are a madman!"

"Am I." Corey was expressionless and in no way ironic. That would have been unprofessional.

"It will melt!"

"I assume so, yes."

"But my *clothes* will get wet!"

Corey dared to guess that she was not referring to the clothing she presently wore. "That seems likely."

Naturally, Corey was only a shapeshifter. He did not have time leap powers, as some specials did, so he had no means of editing the rest of his conversation with Countess Cryo and skipping to the end—the point when she surrendered to the inevitable and spent the rest of her time before nightfall berating her longsuffering goon to pack up her many, many large closets full of clothing faster, faster, *faster* and also more carefully. Corey would have quite liked to be a timeshifter rather than a shapeshifter, if only for that day. He really would have been much happier to skip straight to the part where Countess Cryo had rescued all her beloved clothing and was welcoming Captain Valiant with an evil, villainous cackle.

The ice palace shimmered in the light of a full moon in a clear Hawai'ian sky clustered with stars. It was like one massive, beautiful diamond, descended from the endless night filled with millions of its tiny diamond kin. Countess Cryo was herself decked in a whole swarm of diamonds, and her evening gown glittered along with the copious jewelry.

As predicted, Captain Valiant assigned the battle to his sidekick. Corey sat at the base of the pavilion, looking very basalt, and waited, hoping that Countess Cryo would remember to play her part in the fake death match correctly and not do anything to make Becky—or rather, NitroGirl—suspicious.

NitroGirl was not actually a weak heroic special. She was probably new to the job, and certainly less effusively endowed with powers than Captain Valiant. But she could fight. She had laser swords and some sort of jump boost—not actually flight, but useful for getting around during her battle. She managed to take out enough of the pavilion's pillars that the roof half-collapsed, and Corey rolled himself carefully under the cover of the polyurethane. Not that Captain Valiant was surveying the area. He was mostly engaged with watching the fight, in an attitude that suggested someone ought to supply him with popcorn.

Hidden from sight, Corey shifted into the form of Countess Cryo. He immediately felt certain parts of not-his body affected by gravity in a more-then-usually powerful way. Alarmed, Corey rearranged his structure. He usually merely imitated appearances, and sometimes that meant he got other attributes of matter wrong: weight, temperature, firmness, for example. Corey had originally shifted himself into a copy of Countess Cryo's evening gown that was made of fabric, much as he assumed most clothing was. He had not thought to ask if this was correct, and in fact he was slightly wrong, because Countess Cryo's clothing was undergirded with ice. Corey managed a similar effect with basalt—it was fresh in his memory and helpfully firm, if a bit heavy—and with proper support, not-his body finally resembled Countess Cryo's, as he had seen it.

And not a moment too soon. The Countess had not actually been much of a match for NitroGirl, who didn't seem bothered by cold air and ice and snow attacks. Barely a moment after he was properly ready, Countess Cryo slid under the roof near him, and Corey had to scramble out the opposite side and play his part.

NitroGirl leapt at him and slashed with her laser sword. Corey felt it cut through the basaltic gown just under his ribs, and he converted some of himself into an appropriate display of blood. Grasping the "wound," Corey turned to face the heroic special just in time to get knocked prone. NitroGirl stood above him, sword raised.

She really is too cute for that dimwit…

Corey struggled to focus, Countess Cryo's dying word ready upon not-his lips.

But NitroGirl didn't bring her sword down.

Corey felt vaguely uncomfortable as he waited for the blow. When planning these death battles, he usually didn't schedule long delays at this point. The unexpected red light was troubling to Corey. He didn't need more time to observe NitroGirl up close. Especially not when he needed to remember to call her something really unkind, which he didn't mean at all, in a few seconds.

If she killed him in those few seconds as expected.

"Becky, what are you doing? Finish her!" Captain Valiant's voice broke in upon Corey, somewhat spoiling the moment. Not that he was having a moment. Nobody was having anything of the kind. Becky was just taking a break before killing him, that was all.

But Becky—NitroGirl, rather—dropped her sword to the side, looking complicated and upset about it. "I can't!"

Captain Valiant flew up beside her. "What do you mean you can't? Look, you beat her. You better finish her before she gets up again and does something villainous."

Corey felt suddenly that a screeching cackle would be just the thing here. It was the Countess Cryo way. And yet he hesitated, because he might presently have vocal cords that mimicked hers, but he didn't know how to use them to make sounds like *that*.

"But what has she done that's deserving of death?" Becky countered.

"She killed people!"

"Did she? Are you sure?"

"Well, she must have, she conquered Hawai'i."

"On the way here, Hawai'i didn't look like it had noticed. All I've seen her do is build a big ice thing in a national park—which, okay, not legal, but not really a capital crime either."

Captain Valient stalled out for a minute. Corey subtly tried to clear not-his throat, flexing carefully to see if he could tighten not-his vocal cords enough for a good shrill Countess Cryo contribution to the topic at hand.

"Well...well, what about that guy over there? He's covered in blood! She probably was just killing him!"

Becky glanced at the sidelined goon. "That's pasta sauce," she said.

Corey took a chance. He forced out the best imitation he could give of a Cryo cackle. It sounded a bit weak and wheezy to him. *Doesn't matter, she's supposed to be dying anyway.*

His efforts went mostly unnoticed.

"Look, I'm just saying maybe I don't feel so comfortable with this whole judge, jury, and executioner thing we do. I mean, if they're actively killing people and we can't stop them any other way, that's one thing, but this just seems..." And she looked at Corey.

Corey tried very hard to make not-his eyes flash malevolently, but it came through rather blurry. His vagueness was making a sneaking comeback.

"Well, what else can we do with her? Normal jails can't hold specials. I really think you're just being over-sensitive again, babe."

"I'm *not* over-sensitive at all! I'm not even regular sensitive compared to most people, you're just a—"

"Becks, come on, can't we do this later?"

A harsh sigh. "*Later.* If later ever came, sure, but Valley—"

It was increasingly evident that Corey was not going to get killed on schedule if he didn't do something. So he improvised.

With a sudden shriek—quite good, actually, and certainly an improvement on the cackle—he leapt up and lunged at the heroics. He had not actually seen Countess Cryo manifest an ice sword out of thin air, and he had no certainty that she could actually do that—but Corey could manifest himself into something that *looked* like an ice sword. It seemed apropos.

He slashed a deadly-looking arc at Becky, desperately hoping that they would counter him in time and not wait around to discover that the ice sword was actually less sharp than a butter knife. Luckily, Captain Valiant, though a real thoroughgoing idiot, was actually fairly athletic and well-trained in hand-to-hand combat, as well as having all those special abilities. And, of course, he had his girlfriend to protect.

Corey took a mega-fist right to the torso and sent blood spraying. Then, eager to finish this difficult job, he delivered Countess Cryo's one-word farewell—the male version, for Captain Valiant—and dissolved into dust.

"Ah. That again. Why does that *happen?*" Becky turned to Captain Valiant. "And *you!* How could you just—"

Back in basalt, Corey listened igneously. There was some recrimination, and a number of side issues entered the discussion that did not seem relevant, as topics went, but did seem to be making an encore appearance. The ice palace began to drip water as the temperature around them climbed back up toward 80 degrees. The sun glistened on shiny wet pinnacles, and an ominous cracking sound began. Corey hoped the heroic specials would take their lovers' tiff away with them, because it would be so inconvenient if his client—still hiding under her collapsed pavilion—were crushed by a falling iceberg.

"Okay, you know what, Valley?" Becky's tone brought Corey's attention back sharply. "If that's the way you feel about it, we're done."

Corey's stone heart leapt. *Done?*

"Done? What? Are you *dumping* me?"

"Yup. And if that makes work awkward, I'll resign too. I'll go sidekick for someone else. In fact, let's just make it official. Saves time."

She rocket-jumped away. "Becky! Wait!"

On the warm, sunny slopes of Hualālai, a very wet chunk of basalt morphed into a vague fellow, sitting in a fast-growing creek of melting ice water. Corey gazed expressionlessly at the middle distance—his personal favorite distance. "So they broke up," he murmured.

Then a screeching peal of laughter brought him back to his job. Countess Cryo was furious about her ice palace, and she was expressing herself with heathen decibels—as well as by encasing her waiting goon in ice. Corey stepped up quickly.

"Ma'am, please remember that according to the contract you cannot murder anyone in my presence. It would make me a party to the crime, which the agency does not allow."

The Countess stopped, glared at him, and the ice burst apart. Then she shrieked again. Then she said, "I'm going shopping."

The goon rushed ahead of her, instantly assuming the role of chauffeur.

Corey mumbled to himself, "Someone needs to chill."

———

The jet, alas, had gone on its way, busy transporting other agents.

Corey caught a puddle-jumper to Oahu and had to brave Daniel K. Inouye International Airport. That should have been fine—the layover was only four and a half hours, and there were direct flights from Oahu to Chicago. Unfortunately, it was getting late. Corey had a vague, creeping fear that he knew what was coming.

Indeed, the flight was cancelled—mechanical issues again. Corey got back off the plane and waited at the booking counter for a while.

It was the middle of the night by now, so his options were complicated. If he wanted another direct flight to Chicago, he'd have to spend the night in the airport and fly out in the morning and lose the entire next day between travel and time changes. Otherwise, his shortest layover option was Los Angeles, but Corey knew better than to trust that he'd be able to make a quick connection at that nightmare monstrosity of an airport. His next best option was a red-eye to Phoenix. He'd have a slightly longer layover but could leave Hawai'i almost immediately.

Corey, though a special, was not immune to the universal plague of humanity—that is, the need to be *going* somewhere when in an airport. He shared the common human weakness of loathing the idea of sitting around with nothing to do but wait. He took the connection to Arizona.

Alas, how foolish.

Phoenix Sky Harbor International Airport grounded all flights as temperatures climbed to 120—and they waited until Corey got there before they did it.

Corey was stuck in Phoenix all day.

After dark, when planes could take off again, he found the direct flights to Chicago were full until the next day, which was forecasted to be just as hot. Corey got on the first plane going in a close-enough direction and landed in Salt Lake City, where he spent the remainder of the night. Fortunately, there were three direct flights to Chicago from there, all leaving in the morning, and for once, none of them broke down—not even the one Corey got on. Three and a half hours later, he was finally home.

And late for work.

6

When the bell tinkled at the office on Monday morning, Carol raised a bright and glossy red smile to the person entering. This froze, she blinked, and then Carol busied herself at her computer. The upper and lower slabs of lipstick promptly glued themselves together and stayed that way.

Corey was much darker in complexion than usual—his hair was nearly black. He had two days' worth of stubble on his face, and his expression was sharp and haggard. Carol picked up the inter-office phone to avoid speaking to Corey, whose quick, precise strides headed straight for the back room and the Keurig.

Corey popped a light roast pod into the machine and picked up the forms for his report. Carol sent a cautious glance back through the door and did not interrupt him, even though his client arrived for the interview before he had finished. Only when she saw him sharply place his completed report in the intake pile did Carol rise, swallow, and tap gently at the half-open door.

Black eyes flashed at her.

Carol presented an extraordinarily wide, sweet smile, and a soft and darling tone to match as she held out three new files. "These are your interviews for this morning. I've…raised your rate again, slightly. You're set to depart for Sweden this afternoon. I'm afraid I haven't been able to clear any extra vacation time yet, and the jet is currently in Chile, so—"

Corey's dark tan grew darker, charring toward inky black.

"I'm upgrading your seat to business class. And there's only one very short stop in Reykjavík. And I'll…rearrange some things so that the jet can bring you back."

Corey gave her one slow, speaking look and took the files from her. Then he left for the conference room and his interview. Carol clicked her tongue against bleached white teeth and picked up the inter-office phone. "Eugene?" she said. "Re-run Corey's budget for me. What would it take to get him out of all commercial travel?"

Eugene's phone-voice was incredulous. "You want to put him on priority one for the jet?"

"Is it possible?"

"*No!*" The line clicked dead.

Carol rolled her eyes and stomped down the hall to Eugene's office. Without knocking, she opened his door. "Why not?"

Eugene looked up at her with all the bluntness of his blunt features and pointed a stubby finger at her. "The jet is for the top earners, or for the middle-weights who need to bring support or equipment they can't bring on a normal plane. Everybody else goes only when their schedules match up with a route we're already flying. The problem is, you go giving these specials the idea that it's normal for them to get zipped around the world on a private jet for their work. Then they're disappointed after hiring when it isn't like that."

Carol's smile was rather sharply inverted. "Corey is one of our most popular agents and his time is money. I can't book him for jobs when his days are getting eaten up by fourteen hours in the air."

"The jet isn't a teleporter. It saves a few hours in airports, but it isn't that much faster. And Corey only needs one ticket. Paolo needs three, everywhere he goes. Ronica has to bring her lab, which is insanely expensive or just plain illegal, depending on destination. They bring in profits that reflect the expense, and we save money by just flying them ourselves. You know what jet fuel costs? You bump Corey up to priority one and you'll barely make a profit on his contracts anymore."

Nodding impatiently through most of this, Carol finally held out a staying hand. "I know! Okay, I know. Okay, so—what if I fly him business class from now on, at least?"

Eugene's eyes clicked up to the ceiling for half a second, then back to her. "That'll cut into your profit margin by about 25 percent. Those tickets are ridiculous."

"Still cheaper than the jet."

A huff. "*What* is all this fuss about? What's so terribly wretched about a normal economy-class seat? It's good enough for me!"

Carol smiled tightly in a particularly un-smiley way. Eugene had flown exactly once in his life, as everyone knew—to Bermuda, for a vacation. She did not dignify his complaint with a response. "Could you please run the numbers and get me an annual estimate for upgrading all Corey's commercial flights to business class?"

Eugene directed a short silence at her. Then: "Fine."

"Tha-anks!" Carol hurried back to the front desk.

———

Meanwhile, Corey returned from his interview. His coffee was gone, and he prioritized the Keurig. He needed another.

Suddenly, a filing cabinet released a person into the room. That is to say, a woman turned around and said, "Oh, hello. Corey, right?" when there had appeared to be no one standing at the filing cabinet a moment ago. Corey's hand jerked sharply, but otherwise he did not react.

"Yes. You're new, aren't you?"

"Yup. Camillia."

"That's right. Sorry, it's been a long…" Corey faded out.

"You don't look like yourself," Camillia agreed. She ambled over and stood by him at the coffee station. Leaning one hip against the table, she promptly became a uniform wood-grain walnut veneer color from head to toe. "No offense."

"Quite all right," Corey said, a little too sharply, for him.

"Is the job going all right? Looking at you, I kinda wonder what I got myself into," she joked.

"You'll be all right."

"Mmm. Hope so. Hey," she added, laying out a few forms on the table, "are these right? Carol said I had to sign a few things for new hires, and I think I found the right file folder, but I just want to make sure. I dunno where Carol went."

Corey glanced. "Yeah, those are right. Payroll, client confidentiality, liability release, NDA, company policies…" Corey's voice dropped a degree, "including proper conduct toward heroic specials, and the agreement to maintain your secret identity."

"Man, we really have to have a secret identity? That's so old-fashioned!"

"Only toward heroic specials and the media, really."

"Hmm."

"We don't usually spend much time with them anyway," Corey added, unprompted.

The wood-grain walnut veneer-colored woman tipped her head and regarded him. "You sound bummed about that."

Corey snorted. "That's—!" Then his face paled slightly, and his usual bland expression began to creep in. "Maybe a little." He picked up his coffee and took his paperwork to the couch.

"Wanna talk about it?" Camillia asked, shoving off from the table and following. The walnut veneer slipped away from her, leaving a normal-colored human in normal clothes for a brief moment. Then she flopped down on the couch next to him and promptly turned entirely beige, with that pebbly-pocketed weave pattern. She was all but invisible, nothing but open eyes in a couch, and an open mouth when she spoke.

"It's nothing, really. Just a heroic special I've been hired for a few times. It's sort of worrying, because she's smart, and she might see through my retirement plan, at some point. I should be trying to put her out of commission, or make sure I never come up against her again. But…"

Camillia smiled. "She's probably gorgeous, huh?"

Corey focused on his paperwork. "No. Not at all. But…" He signed a form sharply. "She's cute, I guess."

The old-sofa-patterned face flashed a smiling row of white teeth. "Does she like you at all?"

Corey rolled his eyes. "She doesn't even know who I am. We've only met three times, and two of those times I was a woman, and the other time I was a monster…person…thing."

A hum and a nod. "That can be hot, though."

"It wasn't."

"All right." The beige couch-colored person shape leaned forward. "Why don't you talk to her as yourself next time?"

"If there even *is* a next time," Corey tapped at one of Camillia's papers, "there's still this."

Camillia set the papers on the coffee table and leaned a hand on the surface. That hand and forearm turned black— the color of the coffee table. It was an Ikea. "Look, I know I'm new around here," Camillia said, "but I think this is one of those policies that you can loosen up on. Sure, protecting your secret identity is easier if you never speak to them, but you don't have to be such a martinet. Theoretically you could still keep the secret even if you married one of them. So just talk to her, if you get a chance. It'll do you good."

Corey grunted vaguely. "Will it."

"Definitely." Camillia stood, and the beige weave left her. "Self-doubt is no good for any of us. A little disappointment—you can get over that. *If* it doesn't go well." She shrugged. "But who knows? It might."

Carol came in then, and Corey was vaguely glad she hadn't come back earlier. Camillia handed over her paperwork and left with a cheerful, "Good luck!"

Carol gave Corey a tight smile. She thought he looked a little lighter, a little more like overdone toasted marshmallow rather than charcoal, but she didn't want to reverse whatever process had started bringing Corey back to his inscrutability. "Countess Cryo went well?"

"Mm."

"What's she going to do with her retirement?"

Corey didn't know why Carol asked. She'd see the answer on his paperwork in a minute. "She's opening a craft fro-yo place on the Oahu boardwalk…and running for Senate."

"Huh." Carol nodded, paused, rubbed at the front of a bleached tooth with a fingertip, removing a smear of lipstick. Then she leafed through Camillia's paperwork, and her smile relaxed. It looked almost natural for a minute. "I like this one. Doesn't miss a thing, writes cleanly. She's as good as you are."

Corey nodded. "She's fitting in well around here."

––––––

Eugene's financial report was extremely detailed and mind-boggling, but Carol was not one to be boggled. Carol was a bright plastic smiley face painted on top of a dagger with the mind of a genius tactician. She read the report and made some adjustments.

"I'm raising your rate again, just a bit," she said, leafing through the updated contract, "and your commercial flights will be first class from now on, whenever possible. I think we're doing pretty well with the Zoom interviews, so we'll keep that up. Some clients can't use Zoom due to things like invisibility issues, stuff like that, but we can work those in during the times when you're back in the office. Most clients you can meet with remotely."

Corey listened without expression, scanning the contract. Then, in a monotone, he said, "You still have me circumnavigating the globe."

"Yes, but slower." Carol tapped her projected schedule for the next two weeks. "I'm giving you more time in between jobs. It's not enough to fly back home, but I thought you could just stay where you are and rest up a bit before heading out."

"Stay where?" Corey gave her a blank look. "Going to pay to put me up in a hotel?"

Carol stretched her smile to its biologically improbable limits. "We're adding that to the list of client obligations."

Corey said nothing. His face remained reassuringly expressionless, though Carol hoped she was imagining the slight narrowing of his eyes.

"They always have the space, at least. Even in the low-caliber lairs."

Corey still said nothing. Carol decided not to push it.

"I'll be booking you pretty far in advance, this way," she added. "And I'm going to block out some regular vacation time. I've put a spot here," she indicated, "because I thought if there were any cities you are actually interested in spending some time in, you could list them, and then I could try to work it so that when you have a job there, you get a few days off to stay and vacation. We can maybe work that out once a month, I'm hoping. And every six months you *will* get to come home for a week." She pointed to another clause. "Contractually required."

This time, Corey gave a nice, vague hum. "The rest of the time, I live on the road."

"Looks that way. Your fault for being so popular."

Corey sighed. "You're not asking the clients to put me up for these mini-breaks, though, are you?"

"Well, no, we can't ask that. It's technically vacation time, and most of them probably wouldn't be willing." Carol bit a little dent into her lipstick. "You're making pretty good money, though…"

Corey gave her a flat look. "My bed at home is free to sleep in."

Under the desk, Carol's toe tapped, her sharp heel digging into the flat office carpet. "How about this. We'll cover the hotel room for mini-breaks, you cover food and whatever other costs you incur."

For a long moment, Corey didn't answer. Then, just when Carol was beginning to fear losing her top seller, Corey gave a vague shrug, took the pen, and sharply and precisely signed his new contract.

7

Two weeks around the world, going ever eastward, and Corey wrapped up his inaugural first-class trip with a job in Japan. He landed in Tokyo and got a quick connecting flight to New Chitose Airport in Hokkaido. His next villain was a bit of a recluse, it seemed.

A private helicopter picked him up from New Chitose and took him directly to Rishiri Island. Wikipedia informed Corey that Rishiri was a bird sanctuary, of which it had a great many more than it had humans. The extinct peak of Rishiri-san rose in the center of the little round island—a dream come true for symmetry enthusiasts. In his fly-over, Corey immediately tagged Rishiri as "remote" and "extremely scenic."

Then the helicopter landed on the wildflower-speckled green lawn of a moderately sized traditional Japanese house. The place was in good repair, but had weather-stains to prove it was not new. Corey hopped out of the helicopter and was met by a nice young lady in a maid uniform with her mouth sewn shut.

Corey was a bit uncertain how to respond. The maid said nothing, as might be expected. After a strange moment, she gestured toward the house. Corey nodded vaguely and followed, hoping this wasn't a harbinger of things to come.

Alas for the hardworking retirement agent.

What appeared to be a perfectly normal traditional-style house, both inside and out, revealed its hidden depths in a moment. The maid reached behind a hanging calligraphy scroll; Corey heard a faint *click*, and the floor opened up. Tatami mats dropped a few inches and slid under other mats, and the whole tatami floor parted like a mechanical Red Sea, revealing a sunken staircase.

Beneath the house sprawled a massive underground complex. Corey was undecided on the question of whether it was a labyrinthine dungeon with a spaceship aesthetic or an evil futuristic science lab where the scientists took Halloween very seriously and all got together to decorate for an office party at the end of October. Corey inclined a little bit toward the latter, especially when he discovered that the guards stationed at various doors and corridors were all kigurumi—M16-toting cartoon animal mascots.

As unprofessional as it might have been, Corey would probably have asked a few tactful questions about the facility, but his escort would have been in a difficult position when it came to answering him, so he resisted, out of consideration for her.

Questions continued to percolate as Corey followed the silenced maid deeper into the underground lair. He had not yet actually seen his client's face—during the initial Zoom interview, his client had appeared as a backlit silhouette. This was nothing strange. About 15 percent of Corey's Zoom interviews had chosen the mysterious silhouette so far—optionally with a Darth Vader™ voice filter too. It wasn't worth making a fuss over. Corey could shapeshift into anyone or anything that he saw once, so as long as his clients did eventually drop the mystique, the retirements went fine.

Yet this job, it seemed, contained a high concentration of oddness.

The final chamber the maid led him into appeared to be utterly enormous. It was built around an underground hot spring. But the hot springs themselves were a relatively small, though central, part of the room. The rest was like a small park, containing a traditional onsen, with lighting to imitate the night sky. In fact, the extent of the room was obscured by darkness, so Corey really couldn't estimate the actual size.

In the center, down a mossy flagstone path, Corey found his client lounging in the hot spring as though it were his throne. He was evidently a *he*, though Corey still could not see what his face looked like, because he was wearing a kabuki mask in the bath. By the color of his hair, however, Corey suspected he was not Japanese. He was blond, but not the bottle yellow color of a J-rock star—a natural looking sandy blond.

"Ah, he is here."

And there's that, Corey thought. The words had contained a subtle but distinct Russian accent.

"I understand you know something of my nemesis, Captain Valiant."

Corey was not startled. He already had the paperwork in hand; he knew who would be killing him this time—*again*. He didn't recall revealing to his client that he had encountered Captain Valiant before, though...

"I requested you for this very reason. I know all about the means of blocking his x-ray vision. There is no need to speak of routine matters such as this. I have a unique proposal for you, Shapeshifter-san. Perhaps you will hear me out."

Corey cleared his throat and approached to stand at the edge of the spring, assuming a vague posture, neither overly businesslike nor terribly servile—neither taking charge nor abrogating it. "I beg your pardon, ah—" He opened his file.

"Never mind what you have written there. Call me Batsu, and that is enough."

Corey nodded. "I beg your pardon Mr. Batsu, but unless that mask is, in fact, your face, I feel I should remind you that I cannot take your form and be killed in your place if I have never seen you."

Ever-so-entirely slowly, Batsu raised one dripping arm and snapped his fingers. The wall behind him flickered to life, changing from a display of wooden fence-boards to a screen showing a pretty blonde girl, who began speaking in a tragic voice, her blue eyes as drippy as Batsu in the bath.

"Hello, Brian," she said, with a weak smile. "I don't know if you remember me. In ninth grade—"

Corey let her talk for about a minute. When it didn't seem like the recording was wrapping up any time soon, he vaguely cleared his throat again. "Mr. Batsu, would you be so kind as to explain to me the connection between this girl and your retirement?"

"Can you take her form?"

Corey did not hesitate, not even blandly. "Of course." He had seen enough.

"Then she it is you will be, and you will get her killed."

"Is she—" Corey glanced at his file, "—'The Abominable Cataclysm'?"

"No," the client answered, with a wet shrug. "But Captain Valiant will think so."

Corey had noticed a missing piece here. "Again, pardon me, but the retirement plan I supply, which you requested, usually requires the client—the actual nemesis of the heroic special in question—to engage in a death match with the heroic special. I then swap in and take the final blow, rendering the illusion of your death. But if you are not this girl and you expect me to take this girl's form, it seems like you expect me to handle the entire fight, which is something I cannot do. Apart from shapeshifting, I have no other special abilities. My ability to mimic the special abilities of others is limited to putting up façades. I cannot actually fight."

Batsu snapped his fingers and the screen shut off. Then he rose from the bath and wrapped a yukata around himself. "Come." He indicated the nearby room, open to the patio and the hot spring. Inside was a low table, called a chabudai, with two zabuton for kneeling upon. "Have some tea."

A server in a kimono appeared to make the tea. She was elegant and poised in the traditional clothing, hair, and makeup, though the effect was somewhat spoiled because she, too, had her mouth sewn shut. Corey began to debate whether this was a contract violation. His clients were not allowed to kill or commit atrocities in front of him—and generally the whole idea of retirement indicated that they were done with all that anyway. Usually they cleaned up their misdeeds before his arrival. But the contracts only specified "not making the agent party to criminal activity, see Forms 288733994a–288733994c." Without asking the women about their circumstances and hearing their account, it seemed impossible to determine if this were a contract violation or not—yet.

"I will explain." The client sipped his matcha. "The girl you saw on the screen was my sister. She knew this 'Captain Valiant' since their school days, and she adored him. He refused her. She later developed a tragic terminal illness and died at a young age. I made these recordings beforehand, although she would not say and do everything I wanted, so I have been working on altering and augmenting them with the aid of AI in the years since."

"Ah. Did I see any of the AI work?" Corey asked, mildly curious.

"A tiny adjustment, I think, but not the significant part, no. That is later. My plan is to lure Captain Valiant into a labyrinth I have prepared for him here. He will encounter recordings, reminding him of my sister and his treatment of her. The later recordings show her torturing and killing people—this was the bulk of the AI's work, and I will be curious about how it strikes you, if it seems real enough or not."

"Are the other people also AI creations?"

"Not really." *Sip.* "But their parts were recorded long ago. There is nothing for you to be 'party' to anymore. I and my staff are the only ones here."

Corey was vaguely uncomfortable in the extreme.

"I have created the persona of…whatever that name was you said earlier," he waved a hand dismissively, "in order to lure Captain Valiant here. It will motivate him. The last few recordings present my sister threatening the lives of a great many people, as her vengeance upon Captain Valiant. Before you ask," a staying hand, "no, there are no people in danger. It is a ploy to force him to kill my sister in order to save the people. Only by her death can they survive. Then Captain Valiant is led to the end of the labyrinth, and there you are. You need not fight. You need only be killed."

"I see..."

"Can you cry for your role?"

Corey tipped his head slightly. "If I cannot actually cry, I can shapeshift out some tears."

"The more the better. I would like you to be as lovely and tragic and damaged as possible. I would like him to feel very, very guilty over what he has done, and what he has wrought, and what he must now do."

"I see." Corey glanced at his files. He'd have to get the required paperwork finished somehow, although he wasn't sure all of it applied to this unique situation. "Just to verify, you are actually retiring from villainy, though? You won't be continuing with...whatever you've been doing?"

"Why would I? The purpose will be served."

Perhaps, Corey thought, but he didn't say so. He'd had occasion to observe Captain Valiant's attention span in action, and he harbored some doubts about the heroic's ability to sustain lasting regret. Provided he even managed to notice that he ought to be feeling some regret in the first place.

What he said was, "Well, Mr. Batsu, it appears that most of the information you gave me in our initial Zoom meeting is fabricated, so I'll need to re-do some of this paperwork. As all the information regarding The Abominable Cataclysm is false, considering that individual doesn't exist, let's start there." Thankfully, Corey had his laptop with him, containing all the blank master copies of his various forms. The digitally pre-filled contract he had printed out would have to be scrapped. He opened a new file and entered *Batsu* for the name. The coordinates of the lair were at least the same. "So to start with, I'll need..." Corey glanced up at the kabuki-masked person across from him. "Your special abilities." He blinked, expressionlessly. "Do you even have any?"

His tone had, perhaps, shifted into vaguely skeptical, which was unprofessional. The client regarded him for a long moment, then simply said, "Money."

"Money is not classified as a special ability. Are you a normal, then?"

The client only gave him half a shrug. Corey flipped through his previously filled forms.

"You don't have a referral listed. If I may ask, how did you even hear about our agency?"

The client set his empty cup down quietly and leaned slightly back. "I have complied with your agency's requirement regarding criminal behavior. No one in this facility is being tortured or killed while the agent is present. This is more than enough. I have told you what I want you to do and paid your employer the requested fee. All of this," he swept a hand out, taking in the paperwork and laptop in a gesture, "is your concern, not mine." Rising, he added, "Tea is finished. You may work here if you need to. That," the maid stepped forward, "will take you to the end of the labyrinth when you are ready." And he left.

Corey blankly watched him go, then turned his attention to his favorite distance, the middle distance, and spent a few quality minutes together with it, considering this job.

At Dark Lord Retirement Agency, after Carol, Corey probably knew the forms and procedures and rules better than anyone else. He knew without checking that this job hadn't violated any policies. But there were policies and there was purpose. DLRA hadn't been founded to help rich normals evade justice. It had been founded to help villainous specials evade justice—*Oh wait.*

It's not the same thing, though, Corey told himself. Normals were normal—normal crimes, normal courts, normal punishments. Specials were special, and heroics had decided to start playing judge, jury, and executioner, as someone clever had recently observed. And villains didn't want to die without a trial at the hands of a heroic who thought they deserved it. That was what DLRA was for.

Not this. Not personal vendettas to psychologically punish heroics for what sounded like perfectly normal, non-criminal, human behavior.

Still, it wasn't against any policies. Perhaps it would be, after this. No one had thought to make rules against this. In the meantime, they had already been paid the deposit, and there was a signed contract. Not the final contract, and the name on it was wrong—but then again again again, nobody used their real name in this business anyway.

And really, the middle distance suggested, would it even work?

Corey mused upon this. Given what he knew of Captain Valiant, he suspected that the heroic would not remember some girl he knew (or did he even know her? or did she have a crush on him from a distance?) back in high school. Could Mr. "Out of Sight, Out of Mind" hang on to the memory of some normal girl for that long?

Ultimately, Corey decided, Carol would shred him if he lost the job after flying first class all the way here. He sighed vaguely, eyes roaming over his paperwork. There wasn't much point in filling these out with made-up details. This whole "retirement" job might end up being off-book.

He considered, briefly, whether he ought to make an international call and put it to Carol before doing anything. But upon calculation, Corey found it was the middle of the night in Chicago, and there was no way he'd get an answer. No one had Carol's personal number, and there was no call forwarding for the office phone. The retirement agents kept all hours around the globe, but the receptionist was a strict nine-to-fiver who did not let work bleed into her personal life by one drop.

So Corey stood, finally, leaving his dear friend the middle distance for the time being. He gathered his laptop and paperwork and followed the involuntarily uncommunicative maid to his destination.

8

The arena of confrontation was to be a Japanese school room.

Obviously, Corey was no more inside a Japanese school than he had been at a real onsen, but Batsu's money made quite a convincing presentation of whatever he wanted to display. Corey was not to be outdone by a normal, however, and shifted perfectly into the little blonde Russian girl with pigtails. The maid had taken his laptop and paperwork, for which he was glad. He would have found them a bit cumbersome in his present tiny, frail state.

He knew when Captain Valiant arrived, because an additional screen in the classroom flickered to life and gave Corey a simultaneous presentation of everything the heroic was watching as he progressed through the complex, seeking his nemesis. The early parts of the monologue were rather tiresome, in his opinion, because it mostly involved mundane memories of school days, given an especially saccharine flavor by the heavy dose of nostalgia. Corey found it somewhat nauseous. He didn't listen carefully to that part, but was distracted by the thought: *I didn't know Captain Valiant went to school in Japan. Weird.* He had always seemed too American to have ever been anywhere else. Prom king and high school quarterback somewhere in the Midwest—anyone would have thought so to look at him. *Does he actually speak Japanese, then?* Corey couldn't imagine it.

The recordings shifted as The Abominable Cataclysm began ranting. The cute little pigtail girl began actively harming people. Corey watched with a mixture of repulsion and curiosity. Presumably, Batsu's sister had never actually done any of this, though it was possible that the people being hurt and killed were real. That meant some visual trickery, compositing two shots together. The AI work was probably mostly in the psychotic ranting of The Abominable Cataclysm herself, though. Scrutinizing her very, very closely, Corey could detect the deep fake, but he probably wouldn't have noticed if he hadn't been looking for it. The dying people were distracting him from it. He wondered who they were. He wondered if they had really died or not.

At last, Captain Valiant must be getting near, because The Abominable Cataclysm began her final rant. She had, apparently, utterly filled Sapporo with explosives, which would essentially wipe out the entire capital of Hokkaido and nearly two million people with it. And the detonation sequence was hooked up to her pacemaker—*Pacemaker? Oh, that's right.* There had been something in the middle there about her having to get a pacemaker for her heart trouble, which was apparently Captain Valiant's fault, somehow. So in short, every beat of her heart was ticking the clock down for the people of Sapporo.

Oh I see, Corey thought. Then: *But wait…why am I dissolving into dust, then? She's not even a special.*

Suddenly, Corey became extremely curious—for totally professional reasons—about whether or not Captain Valiant had managed to patch things up with NitroGirl and retain his sidekick. Becky wouldn't buy this for a minute. Corey wasn't sure even Captain Valiant could be so dumb.

He didn't have time to ask. The school room door slid open, and Captain Valiant entered.

First, he was alone. *Thank goodness.*

Second, he was crying. *What?*

Corey had been working on tweaking not-his form to best imitate the manic look the little pigtail girl had acquired by the end of the recording; at the sight of Captain Valiant in tears, he was so startled he went momentarily blank.

"Kin-chan..." Captain Valiant gave a huge sniffle and wiped his nose on a Spandex sleeve. Then, while Corey was processing the possibility that Captain Valiant *might* actually speak Japanese and, if so, might use it—and if he went to school with this girl, presumably she knew Japanese too, and what was Corey going to do if called upon to converse in a language he didn't know?—Captain Valiant crossed the room and bent down and hugged him.

Corey's present form was considerably smaller than Captain Valiant's, so the experience, for him, was mostly a face full of oversized heroic pectorals. Captain Valiant hugged the little blonde pigtail girl and sobbed. Corey felt him shaking with those sobs and blanked out for a moment, left adrift by the whole situation.

A huge, heroic hand cupped the back of not-his head and petted not-his blonde pigtails. "Kin-chan...I'm sorry. I'm so sorry."

Corey didn't reply. He was vaguely trying to scratch his way back toward the role he was supposed to be playing for this job he was getting paid to do. He didn't know how to handle Captain Valiant being devastated. He didn't want to try.

The still-crying heroic pulled back just enough to kneel and meet not-his eyes with a snotty, tear-mottled, bright red wet face. "Don't do this, Kin-chan. Please. I'm so sorry. Please, please stop now."

Corey grasped at the thread of memory that told him how this girl was supposed to have been talking a minute ago. "Never!" he rasped, as poisonously as he could.

"Kin-chan, don't make me...please. For me. Remember? It's Shiro."

If there was one thing Corey knew, it was that he couldn't let this job turn into a conversation. The emotional pleading had to stop now. Anyway, this girl Corey was depicting had been dead for years. It was a wonder Captain Valiant hadn't heard about her passing, but regardless, the heroic was alone in his tragedy. "Kin-chan," or whatever her name had been, wasn't here to be softened by nostalgic affections.

The whole job was a bluff, and the only thing Corey could think to do was to push it even further. Raising not-his little hands, he began: "Ten, nine, eight..." folding down fingers as he went, and trying to keep that manic look on not-his face. "Seven..."

"Kin-chan!"

"Six..." *Please buy this. Come on. You're really not very smart.* "Five..."

And then Captain Valiant stabbed Corey in the heart.

Oh thank goodness.

"F-Four..." Corey managed, manifesting blood from his mouth and chest. Then, voiceless, he smiled, and smiling, died.

Captain Valiant clung to not-him, sobbing, and Corey gladly escaped into dust.

When he was free, Corey reconstituted himself as a fly on the wall and waited, but it seemed that Batsu's plan had really hit home. Captain Valiant sat on the floor of that school room crying, and he didn't seem likely to stop. From the stammering things he said through his tears, Corey learned far more than he had ever wanted to know. He learned that Captain Valiant had always regretted losing touch after high school; that he and "Kin-chan" had been the only two non-Japanese at their school; that he had always regarded her as his little sister; that he couldn't return her feelings, and yet he loved her more than almost anyone else.

Corey finally buzzed quietly out of the room, unable to eavesdrop any longer. He found the maid, returned to his own form, and then apologized for giving her the silent fright of her life. Then: "I'll meet Batsu as soon as possible and wrap this up. If he's busy right now," since Captain Valiant was still present and suffering for his amusement, "I'll wait wherever is most convenient."

The maid nodded and took him back to the onsen, and he had another elegant tea served to him. Corey had to wait about an hour, and he redeemed the time by writing up a short survey of questions regarding consent and asking the two ladies to fill it out for him. He had to use translation software to get it into Japanese for them, but they complied and gave satisfactory answers. Corey did not ask *why* they consented to their treatment; it was only his job to verify that they *did*. Contracts required no crimes in his presence. As long as there was no involuntary detention or non-consensual maltreatment, there was no crime for him to report.

Everything was above-board. The agency was paid, Corey did the same job as always, and he had nothing to file against Batsu on his paperwork.

And he was never, *never* going to do this again.

9

Corey took his mini-vacation in Hokkaido. There was a short ferry from Rishiri Island over to nearby Rebun Island—less symmetrical and even less populated, noted on Wikipedia for alpine flowers. Corey sat by the sea in perfect quiet and peace for two days, enjoying the remote north of Japan. Then he took another ferry back to Wakkanai, on Hokkaido, and got a train to Sapporo.

In Sapporo, Corey had a decision to make. His first-class flight direct to Chicago would depart from Tokyo. He could take a quick flight from Hokkaido to Tokyo—either a later one, after spending a little time touring around Sapporo, or an earlier one, leaving him time afterward to see a little bit of Tokyo. Or—Japan was the land of trains. He could spend a few extra hours and go south by train. It would use up most of his free time, but the trains were especially nice, and Corey was tired of flying.

He took the train.

Overall, he enjoyed the ride, especially all the scenery of Japan's countryside. However, he did get a little confused when he had to change trains to the express in Aomori, and he missed his train and had to take a later one. As a consequence, Corey also missed his flight and had to reschedule for the next day. He kicked himself a little bit over that, but compared to most of his travel nightmares, it was a relatively mild crisis and easily fixed. He paid for his own hotel in Tokyo, since Carol hadn't been planning on covering another overnight for him. He could have slept in the airport for free, but there are some things in this world that no one wants, even for free.

Shortly before dawn, Corey Zoom called Carol, managing to catch her before she left the office for the day. He had to discuss the paperwork with her.

Carol clicked her tongue and said, "Let's do this. Send in what you have. I know it's not much. He still signed the contract, the NDA, and the liability forms, right?"

"Yes, but he gave no real information, and I'm pretty sure he's not a special at all."

"I'll get someone to look into it. 'Batsu' will be blacklisted, obviously, just in case he doesn't stay 'retired.' But we'll try to find out what we can so he can't pull this kind of stunt again."

"What if someone else tries it?"

Carol frowned. "You mean a normal?"

"He found out about us. What if others do?"

Carol's eyes went for a little wander over a few drop ceiling tiles. "Well, we're not really *for* normals, but if they can *pay*... I mean, we can't have all this secrecy and false info in the future, though. That's for sure."

Corey remained vague in face and voice, though his foot tapped sharply out of sight and the backs of his hands and arms tanned a few shades darker. "But we'll do 'retirements' for normals if they have enough money?"

Carol's eyes remained adrift. "I don't know. We'll have to have a planning meeting, and if it ever does come up again, we'll look into it pretty thoroughly before we take the contract..."

"I don't retire normals." Corey cut through Carol's lingering ellipses with a punctual full-stop. He remained blank and flat, but there was nothing vague about what he said. "I retire specials. Normals can go to normal prison if they've done wrong. Specials get a hero on their tail and we know how that always ends. They retire because they don't want to die. They don't necessarily deserve to retire, but they don't necessarily deserve to die, either. What I mean is—*I don't retire normals*. Rich people can already do whatever they want. I'm not helping with that. You take their money if you choose. But if you do, I'll quit."

Corey ended the call before Carol could respond.

Then he closed up his laptop and left for the airport. He arrived good and early and had leisure to ask about the plane and learn that it was running on schedule and having no mechanical problems. His flight was expected to be on time.

Corey sat at his gate as the crowd of passengers slowly gathered, and he reviewed his paperwork. It irked him how incomplete it was, and what he did have was blatantly false. He finally gave up and sent it in as it was. Carol would have to deal with it.

Then, as he waited, Corey saw a familiar-looking girl join the crowd at his gate. Something in his stomach gave a vague lurch before his mind had quite finished deciding that, yes, that was Becky, also known as NitroGirl. It was her in a hoodie rather than Spandex, but it was her. And she was apparently taking this flight.

This impossible good luck was exactly the sort of thing upon which even the most sanguine of temperaments tended to look askance. Corey was not sanguine. Corey generally tested as phlegmatic—at times a little choleric.

However, the fates took no notice of personality tests, and they arranged matters as they best preferred. And today, they best preferred that Corey should fly from Tokyo to Chicago without any delays or complications, and that he should sit next to a girl called sometimes Becky, sometimes NitroGirl.

"Here," Corey said, interposing a hand between the further corner of her carry-on and the edge of the overhead compartment. Thus adjusted, the carry-on slid neatly into place, and Becky smiled.

"Thanks."

Corey nodded vaguely and took his seat.

Both of them fastened safety belts and put phones in airplane mode and adjusted their seats and generally did all the usual pre-flight stuff. During this, there was no particular reason to talk, so Corey didn't. Then the flight attendants began their usual circus sideshow, and then takeoff happened, and then that wonderful first-class service kicked in. Becky seemed a little startled by it.

"First time in first class?" Corey asked.

"Yeah," she breathed. "My last flight was a *nightmare*, like you wouldn't believe, and the airline made a huge mess of it all, so they upgraded me. Normally I'd be back there in the chicken coop somewhere."

Corey certainly knew about nightmare flights. But he would rather turn to other topics. "So are you going home now?"

"Not home. Next stop."

"Next stop? So Tokyo was a stop, and Chicago is another? Where else?"

"Oh gosh, lots of places. Milan and St. Petersburg and Dubai and Sydney. Oh and London; that was first. And I was supposed to hit Cairo, but things happened and that didn't work out."

Corey was perhaps a little less awed than Becky might have anticipated. "Where after Chicago?" he simply asked.

"*Then* home."

"Ah."

"Houston."

"Oh nice." Corey was vaguely glad she had offered that detail. He didn't like to feel that he was grilling her. "That's a lot of travel. Work-related?"

Becky sighed. "Well, yes and no. Basically, I used to travel for work—um, not by flying commercial, though. I was, uh, kind of a sidekick. Professionally."

Corey hummed vaguely.

"I quit that, or retired maybe, whatever. Right now I'm traveling around because me and a couple other people with special abilities got this idea to start sort of like an international big brothers/big sisters organization. Like a mentoring program for young specials. Their social and educational needs are a bit different from normal kids, and you know, depending on where they're born, things can be really rough. The organization is still in the formation phase right now. I'm kind of recruiting." She shrugged, smiling.

"Mentorship for people with special abilities?"

"Mm-hmm."

"Is it your goal to prevent specials from becoming villains?"

Becky shrugged. "I mean, yes, that's definitely part of it. But we think everyone needs some mentorship, even heroes. Heroes have their own issues, and a lot of it comes from not having anyone who can support them in the areas where they're different. And then there are lots of people with special abilities who don't have enough power to really excel in that kind of career path, whether heroic or villainous, but they have enough to be misfits in the rest of the world. Maybe what they're really cut out for is nursing, or being a tax accountant, or starting a small business in their local community. But you wouldn't believe how complicated that gets if you happen to have been born with the ability to turn invisible."

"You might be surprised," Corey murmured.

"That's what we want our big brothers and big sisters to help out with—navigating those complications so that hopefully specials can have a normal, productive life. And if they have high levels of ability and want to go pro, ideally they'd be doing things like helping rescue people from natural disasters, things like that. Not that we expect to see the end of all villains forever, but you know, we just want to improve the current situation, which is really too chaotic."

Becky was a hand-talker when she got going, Corey noticed. It was a dangerous thing to be, when you were holding a glass of first-class-flight champagne, but Becky navigated fluid dynamics marvelously and ended her elevator speech with a sip of unspilt prosecco. Then, without warning, she sneezed, and her mastery of the glass in hand failed slightly, sending a tiny shower of champagne over her own nose, chin, and lap. "Oops!"

Corey was quick to swoop to the rescue with the offer of napkins. Becky dabbed at herself, laughing. "This stuff always makes me sneeze. I'm really more of a beer girl, but you know, also kind of a beer snob, and they didn't have anything I wanted to—oh gosh, and you know what else? I ramble like crazy when I drink, sorry about that." As far as Corey's present tally, which was quite accurate, Becky had sipped three times. Her recent spill had lowered the level of drink in her glass by as much as all her drinking so far.

She may not have been much of a superhero, but she was super, *super* cute.

"My name's Becky, by the way." She held out a hand. "Better get that taken care of, so we're not introducing ourselves at the *end* of a twelve-hour flight."

"Corey," Corey said, taking her hand. *Twelve hours*, he thought, and he smiled. It was a small smile, but there was nothing vague about it. "Actually…we've met."

EPILOGUE

The bell tinkled as the horned demon in the ninja outfit left, his appointment reminder card in hand. Carol's radiant customer service smile immediately dropped as her face relaxed, and she automatically reached for the tube of lipstick. A smile like hers required *constant* upkeep.

With a fresh coat of red paint on, Carol returned to the back room and picked up the report she'd left on the top of her intake tray. It was Lucy's, and it reported that Mr. Reichenbacher had "retired" successfully and vanished. Mr. Reichenbacher was a normal—a very, *very* rich one. Lucy didn't care, Eugene *definitely* didn't care, and Carol only cared that he had been upfront with them in every detail and he paid in full and on time.

But she knew who *would* care.

Just back from his latest two-week tour of planet earth, Corey sat on the old couch filling out reports. He hadn't heard about Lucy's assignment yet; he would eventually, but that wasn't the problem right now.

"So…the new schedule is working for you?" Carol began, carefully.

Corey didn't look up. "It's all right."

"Your first full vacation is coming up. Got plans?"

Corey paused and raised his eyes, but not to Carol. He found his old friend the middle distance and communed with it for a moment, then smiled. "Yes," he said, and Carol suffered a chill of dread.

These last five months, Corey had been acting extremely weird, and Carol didn't know how to handle it. She knew how to handle an upset Corey, and she was an old pro at working with normal Corey, whose blankness threw most other people off. This Corey—she had no idea. It was almost like he was *happy* or something. She had no idea how a happy Corey would take this.

"Okay, well, here's the thing. After your vacation, there's a client who requested you."

"Mmm?"

"It's a bit different. Not really a retirement."

"Mm."

Corey didn't look at her, but in his sudden stillness, Carol felt the turn of his focus like a laser beam. She stretched her well-coated lips into a conciliatory murder-smile. "She's a normal, but she's not a criminal escaping justice. More of a minor princess who wants to run away from home and has a dramatic streak a mile wide."

Very calmly and blankly, Corey looked up at her and said nothing. Carol torpedoed ahead, going for broke.

"She can pay, and she wants to fake her death and go off on adventures. She's seen too many movies or something, because she's absolutely determined to dissolve to dust for her staged 'death.' She's been honest about all the details, and I've investigated her. She really hasn't done a thing wrong. And I'm certain I can even go so far as to charge her double and she'll pay it. But she *has* to have *you*."

Carol was already braced, waiting for Corey's coloring to darken or his features to sharpen. None of that happened. Corey listened, then turned his gaze back to the middle distance. He was really getting friendly with that distance these days, and it kept making him smile. He smiled now, and Carol's jaw almost dropped. It was only her lipstick gluing her top and bottom lip together that kept her from making a most ridiculous expression.

"Do you know how she heard about us?"

Carol didn't trust her jaw muscles yet; she left matters up to her lipstick and did not open her mouth. "Mm-mm."

"So we do take normals for clients, when they can pay." He glanced at her. "Been taking any others?"

Carol's fingernails scraped lightly at the file in her hands. She resisted the urge to hide it behind her back. "Mmmmm…"

Corey raised his eyebrows. Carol had never seen him do that before, ever. She swallowed. "Mm-hmm."

"Okay." Corey nodded. Carol, not knowing what this meant, had a dizzy spell and subtly grabbed the edge of the desk to steady herself. "Well, your normal princess is not going to get what she wants, and I resign."

Her worst fears realized, Carol shut her eyes and dropped into a chair. The chair caught her well enough, but it was unhelpful as far as solving this urgent dilemma. Carol was on her own, now. She quickly rallied, desperate not to lose one of her most popular retirement agents. "Never mind! Never mind what I said, there's no princess, I take it back!"

Corey shrugged—a naturally vague gesture, but not this time. It was plainly dismissive. "I still resign. You want to offer services to normals. You knew it would come to this." Crisply, he signed his report and began stacking all the forms in the correct and perfect order. "Actually, I saw this coming since Batsu. To be honest, I've been using my free time between retirements to do a little moonlighting. The international travel has been very useful lately."

Carol sat up straight. "Moonlighting? Doing what?"

Another small but by no means vague smile. "Recruiting." He rose, approached, and held out his reports to Carol. "Don't worry about it. I'm resigning anyway. It was inevitable. Parting ways, no hard feelings, thanks for everything."

It couldn't have been clearer. There was really nothing Carol could do to keep him. She sighed, taking the beautifully thorough reports and accepting her loss. Corey headed toward the door.

"So what are you going to do now?" she asked in parting, her lipstick making a rueful twist.

Pausing with his hand on the door, Corey gave her one more inexplicable smile. "I'm going to help save the world," he said, and then he was gone.

RENT-A-GHOST

1

On the farthest end of the old strip mall, where the weeds grew thickest and tallest through the cracks in the parking lot—that's where the empty storefront was. The one next to it was empty too, but the half-obliterated sign for Joe's Pizza was still there. And next to that was a used bookstore; and next to that was a dingy nail salon; and next to that was an insurance agency; and next to that was a dollar store. Sometimes there were cars parked over there, and the weeds got crushed under-wheel before they could get too far. But down at the far end, down by the empty storefront without even a sign left to show what had once been, the weeds were breaking up the asphalt—building mountains and cutting canyons in the blacktop fields.

The grass growing between the sidewalk cracks was undisturbed upon the threshold, for the door had long gone unopened. The windows had metal shutters down, and there were never lights on because, for all anyone knew, there was nothing there. Old Mr. Adamson at the bookstore didn't know any different. He certainly didn't know that the phone line to the empty store was still active; far less did he know that it was active because someone had rewired the lines to hijack his telephone. He didn't wonder that he never got calls. He never had gotten any.

And the old rotary phone in the empty store might be loud as anything, but it was still divided from the bookstore by the empty pizzeria, and old Mr. Adamson didn't hear well anyway. When that phone rang, no living soul was there to hear it.

The one who did hear it was rather doughy-looking fellow. At the piercing sound of the ring he appeared, drifting through the wall of the back room, or maybe down through the ceiling. He mumbled his "coming, coming" to the screeching phone, settled down more or less on the counter next to it, and promptly shoved his head into the device. The ringing ceased.

A mild voice could be heard in the empty room, apparently coming from the telephone-headed apparition. "Acme Rent-a-Ghost, specters, poltergeists, and astral bodies, this is Chester, how may I help you?"

"Hello. I need an old lady ghost who can knit, and—"

"One moment, please. Will this be a short-term or a long-term rental?"

"I don't know. Probably at least six months. Is that long term?"

"Yes sir, that is definitely long term. Our short-term rentals are for specific events, usually one day, no more than a couple appearances over a weekend. It sounds like you're looking to book a residential ghost."

"Yes, residential, definitely. Maybe for more than six months, if possible."

"That's quite a long-term rental, sir," Chester suggested, reaching up to scratch the side of the phone thoughtfully. "We do charge a lower rate since it would be by the week rather than hourly, and your rental would basically be a live-in specter, but I should warn you that she can't be present and visibly manifesting twenty-four-seven. She'll have to leave for occasional short-term work, and daytime visibility is never guaranteed."

"Oh that's fine, perfectly. And money is no object. But it's very important that she have the correct specifications. Especially her face."

"We can certainly adjust facial features—within limits. You will need to provide us with some good photographs of what you're looking for."

"No problem, I've got all that."

"Okay, then can I get the dates for your rental?"

Chester stretched out an arm and began to scribble notes in the dust of the countertop with his translucent, pudgy finger. "Mm-hmm...mm. Yeah. Okay." After accumulating a little set of details, he concluded the call with: "We'll need you to bring your photos to the interview with Midi, and she'll have the rental agreement for you to sign and you pay the deposit then. And she can go over the details of your haunting and answer any further questions. Yes. All right, nine-thirty tomorrow. Yes. Thank you for calling Acme Rent-a-Ghost, have a nice day."

Removing his head from the telephone, Chester seemed to sigh and rubbed his neck. "Taking calls puts such a crick in my ethereal essence," he moaned.

"I'm not surprised," a scrannel voice responded. "You have dreadful posture."

Chester had evidently not been addressing himself to the newcomer, who was presently rising out of the floor. At the sound of her voice, Chester did not jump or yelp, but his softly glowing outline momentarily expanded outward, edges fritzing into ragged zigzags before easing back into his smooth curves. "I wish you would knock a few times before you do that," he mumbled.

In the most dignified manner imaginable, she replied, "I am *not* a poltergeist, young man."

"I died four hundred years before you were born," Chester grumbled.

"But you only lived a score of years, whereas *I* lived *five* score and three." With this definitive riposte, she manifested a large hat and spectral hatpins and began the arrangement of such. "I am going out. I simply cannot abide society of such quality."

"Ah, Mrs. Amelia Gladstone?" She paused, turning her rigidly upright form slightly to regard him. "We may have a long-term job for you. Depending upon Midi's assessment tomorrow."

Primly: "If you expect me to take up residence elsewhere, make certain that the ceilings are not below ten feet, the windows are not full west, the kitchen is not smoky, the rooms are not damp, and there *must* be a drawing room." She buttoned the wrists of her gloves. "Houses these days. Scandalous things." And with that, Mrs. Amelia Gladstone drifted through the front wall and vanished from Chester's sight—and from all sight, for it was eleven-thirty in the morning on a sunny, late-winter day. No spectral being, regardless of their power, grudge, or dignity, would be visible just now.

Chester displayed no reaction to this, simply watched her go and then turned his morose gaze upon the telephone. One might have wondered that Mrs. Amelia Gladstone could be so selective when her alternative was living in an abandoned unit in a strip mall—but Chester had long accepted this as one of the facts of death. One might have pondered which fellow-resident had caused the old lady's frustration to boil over—but Chester already knew it was bound to be one or both of the children. Mrs. Amelia Gladstone could not abide rowdy children, but neither of the resident child-ghosts had been born under her own "seen and not heard" era, and it was too late to correct their upbringing now.

No, Chester did not bother with these subjects. He was mostly occupied with the necessity of presently sticking his head back into the telephone and calling Midi. When the upper half of a little girl's face appeared through the floor, he did not turn to look.

"Is she gawn?"

"Mm."

A giggle from one, followed by a sigh from the other.

"Jemmie 'n me gawt her propers."

"I gathered." Then, without paying any more attention to the girl, and with a semblance of a deep breath, Chester stuck his head back into the telephone.

Midi's phone buzzed, and she quickly slurped up her mouthful of noodles and stuck her chopsticks in the bowl to free her hand. She thumbed the green icon while swallowing heavily. "Chester?" she said, through the half of her mouth she had emptied. "An appointment? Okay. Yeah, of course."

Midi whipped a fine-tipped marker out of her pocket protector and began to jot notes on the inside of her forearm. Having scrawled the salient details, she replied, "You probably want me to rent out Gladstone, if I can?" Chester's answer was unquestionably affirmative. "I'll see what I can do." That being more of less the end of the call, Midi prepared to hang up, but was stayed by a question. "Eating? Yeah I was eating. …What? Jjajangmeon, why? …Uh, okay, bye." She ended the call and set her phone down on the coffee table, returning to her noodles with a muttered, "Asks that every time…"

One the other side of town, Chester pulled his head out of the telephone and rubbed at his cricked ethereal essence with a wistful sigh.

Midi returned half of her attention to her noodles and the other half to the livestream on her TV.

Cousins Warwick Smith III clutched his latte in front of himself in a defensive way as he stared at the girl taking a seat across from him. She dumped an armload of things onto the table while apologizing: "Sorry I'm late, my scooter wouldn't start." The tiny café table was immediately half-buried in a pile of books, file folders, a tablet, a jacket, a Mickey Mouse pencil case, massive noise-cancelling headphones, an empty travel mug, and an ancient Tupperware® with a sandwich in it. Cousins Warwick Smith III gingerly extended two fingers, tucked them over the rim of his little plate, and tugged it back toward himself to rescue his muffin. "Be right back," the girl added, grabbing up her travel mug. She passed the counter, waving the mug at them and calling, "Just hot water!" The bored teenager ignored her.

This was the picture Cousins III was given some forty-five seconds to study, before the girl returned with her water:

Short, skinny, definitely Asian, but her speech had sounded native English to the final degree, so probably only of Asian descent. Hair gone on some kind of style holiday; big glasses; bright pink lipstick. A t-shirt covered by an oversized plaid flannel long-sleeved shirt with a pocket protector containing pens. Below that, a floor-length white skirt and combat boots.

As the dreaded creature turned back to him and approached, Cousins III had the further opportunity to notice neon salmon nail polish and a sparkly silver star sticker upon one temple. He felt a bit queasy.

"Okay, so you're the customer renting an old lady ghost, right?" The strange creature was talking even as she sat. Cousins III maintained his coffee-and-muffin defensive barricade. The girl perched cross-legged on the chair and flipped open a file, "Cousins...Cousins? Warwick Smith the Third?" She gave him an odd look. "That's your name?"

Cousins III cleared his throat, but was stalled for a moment as the strange creature pulled three little packets out of her pocket protector and emptied them into her hot water—two were clearly instant coffee, and the other appeared to be cherry Kool-Aid®.

"That is...my name." Cousins III summoned his ancient Norman heroism and dared to ask, "Are you...Midi?"

"Mmm," the girl nodded while sipping her—whatever that was.

A tormented note entered his voice as he asked, "What on earth are you drinking?"

Midi looked at him like she was becoming mildly concerned for his sanity. "Um, coffee?" She grabbed her

Tupperware® and produced a peanut butter and jelly sandwich. She angled herself to put her back to the employees behind the counter and hide her food. "Hope you don't mind, but it's the slow season for ghost rentals and the food here, while nice, is really overpriced, so." With a mouthful of sandwich, she added, "You bring your pictures?"

Cousins III reached for his phone. "Yes, um, I have them. When I talked to the guy on the phone, he said the ghost could appear like this?" He gingerly extended his phone with the correct pictures ready to be swiped through. Midi chewed and duly swiped. She nodded.

"This should be okay. Basically the ghosts are able to shift their appearances, but not too much. Or, I should say, if they try to shift into something completely different, it's really hard and they can't hold it for long. But an old lady ghost can make herself look like a slightly different old lady, no problem. Then again, you're asking to rent her for..." She flipped over a form in her file folder, "...*six months?*" Midi gaped at him. "Are you rich?"

Cousins III blinked, somewhat taken aback, like all members of his race, by the gauche inquiry. "I guess so," he said after a minute. Midi continued her gape. Cousins III added, "I mean, I don't own yachts and private jets and that sort of thing, but I can afford this. I feel that this is really important and valuable, if the ghost can appear just like this. And if she knits."

"Well, she knits, sure. She'd be offended if you asked her that, though. It'd be like asking someone if they know how to walk."

"I see."

She pulled out her own phone. "Here, send these to me." As he added her contact and sent them, Midi asked, "So who is she?" pointing to the pictures.

"Oh...my grandmother." Cousins III explained, in more detail, what he'd told the receptionist. "She died recently, and my grandfather is...not okay without her. She used to promise him that she'd hang around and wait for him if she went first." He sighed. "But then she'd turn around and whisper to me that she was only joking, and she was going to go get reincarnated as soon as possible because she couldn't wait to start skiing again. She used to ski all the time, before her hip made her give it up." He frowned at himself for talking too much. "Anyway, I don't know how long my grandfather will last. Right now he seems like he won't make it to next week, but the doctors don't see anything especially wrong with him. I'm hoping if he can have my grandmother's ghost with him, he'll perk up a bit. Then, who knows how long he might last?"

Nodding and swallowing, Midi said, "Gotcha. Okay. Well, if you're fine with the cost, our ghost can manage the appearance. What I'll need from you today then, besides the deposit and the signed contract, is a detailed description of behaviors for your rental ghost. Like, you mentioned knitting—okay, but mannerisms and preferences and her favorite things and spots in the house and all that. Generally we don't go into conversational topics with a haunting like this. I mean, ghosts can talk, of course, but people are usually fine believing in just a visual apparition that doesn't speak, unless they've had much personal contact with ghosts."

"I'm sure he's never seen one in his life. I don't know why he believes that my grandmother will appear, actually. Maybe it's just that he wants it so much."

"Mmm. Could be, could be. Anyway, our ghost will basically be a silent, residential apparition for the rental period. So give us a good, thorough description of how she should act in order to convincingly play your grandmother."

"Sure. Um, you want me to—?"

"Oh, I have a form you can write it on, if you want, or I can just record you talking, if that's easier." Midi extended her phone.

"I don't write that well," Cousins III admitted, accepting the phone. Midi flipped through the paperwork while devouring her sandwich and her offense against coffee. Cousins III mentioned everything he could think of that his grandmother would do, occasionally signing on a dotted line when Midi prompted him to. After his narration was done, he paid the deposit and the first month's rent by transfer.

Midi, examining her phone, said, "Your grandfather's house looks nice." She glanced up. "Just Googling the address. Um, sorry for the question, but is the house damp at all?"

Cousins III was confused, but not to the point of showing it. "No, I don't think so. It seems very dry to me."

Midi nodded. "You don't happen to know how high the ceilings are, do you?"

Cousins III approached a little closer to the point of showing his confusion. "A little high? I really don't know."

"Is there a drawing room?"

Cousins III was finally overcome by his rising confusion and faintly frowned. "I guess there's a sitting room you could call that. May I ask why?"

But Midi just gave him a cheerful and cryptic shrug. "Just trying not to ruin my ghost."

That appeared to be the end of the matter, and as Midi's sandwich and her offense against coffee had met their own ends already, it was now also the end of the meeting. Midi stood and began to gather up her pile of arm-loading things, all while shaking Cousins III's hand and thanking him for his business and promising to be in touch.

She disappeared through the glass front door, and Cousins III sighed in relief and begin to pick at his poor, disregarded muffin.

Outside, Midi tapped at her phone and waited for the call to connect. Then: "Good news, Chester. Gladstone is booked for the next six months."

In the empty strip mall unit, Chester sighed in relief, no longer bearing a grudge over the call. A few moments of his head in the telephone were worth it for the news that Mrs. Amelia Gladstone would be departing from their residence for half a year.

2

Hijacking a phone line was one thing; leeching electricity was another. The bookstore did not use a great deal of electricity—even the signage did not light up. The ghosts had decided that the only thing to do was to leech very little at first, and increase the amount so slowly that the bookstore proprietor would regard the incremental increases on his electric bill as simply the usual steady rise of prices.

By this rule, after Midi brought in the old TV, they only watched it for five minutes a day, at first. They were now up to twenty minutes, and could almost watch an entire episode of a sitcom. It was about as thrilling as death could get, when there wasn't any work and they were stuck in an empty strip mall unit at all hours every day.

"I swear to you, dude, I was the one who turned it on yesterday! It's your turn today!" The skinny teenager was shrill and adamant.

"Oh, but I say! Dash it!"

"Your turn, your turn!" Jemmie bounced.

This was the only difficulty. Someone had to turn the TV on, and whoever did would not be able to watch that day, except the dingy backward reflection of the screen in an old mirror.

The rest of the company agreed, and Lord Watley succumbed to the tyranny of the proletariat. Moustache drooping, he hefted up his weightless, ponderous bulk and waddled over to the TV. Then, with old-world dignity, he stood inside the object, becoming now a TV with ghostly arms and legs and a morose head. The black screen flickered to life—after first producing some black and white static, despite the fact that it was a digital TV and had none of the analog mechanisms to produce analog snow.

Then, at last, the show was showing, and Lord Watley glumly stared at the shoddy reflection in the mirror while the rest of the ghosts gathered around and settled in to watch their sitcom.

Chester popped in suddenly, rushing through the wall. "Did I miss anything?"

Polly pointed at the screen. "That one there just see'd an old schoolmate she don' like and she's hiding, see?"

"Oh good, okay." Chester settled in to watch.

Nearly half an hour later, when Lord Watley removed himself from the TV with stately grandeur, someone—perhaps the skinny teenager—asked what Chester's call had been. "Oh, yes. A booking. I need to call Midi."

"Who is it for?"

"*For whom* is it," Lord Watley intoned. No one heeded.

"Oh, nearly anyone. Midi will choose. I'd better call her." And Chester passed through the wall back to the telephone.

Midi waited outside the residence of Mr. Cousins Warwick Smith, Sr. with Mrs. Amelia Gladstone. It was late evening, and Mrs. Amelia Gladstone could be seen if she wished, but they were waiting for Cousins Warwick Smith III. At present she was invisible, and Midi appeared to be talking to herself.

"Remember? Kitchens aren't smoky anymore. No one cooks on a fire, at least not indoors. And you can see that the house faces southeast. Any windows on the west side will not get much sun through those trees. And I checked with the housing authorities, and the ceilings are, in fact, ten feet."

"With all that shade, it's sure to be damp," Mrs. Amelia Gladstone said, invisibly.

"I have the customer's assurance that the place is quite dry. It's an elderly man's home, and he's well-off. He wouldn't live in a damp house."

"Well." A sniff. "Who, of any quality, would?"

"If I read the floor plans right, that's the drawing room there," Midi added, pointing to a window.

"One certainly hopes it is suitable."

During this exchange, a black Lexus pulled up in front of the house. Cousins III got out and began to approach Midi with a slightly odd gait—two steps slow and hesitant, three quick and eager, like some sort of improvisational tango. Just then, Midi's phone rang.

Midi answered with, "Chester? Sorry, can it wait? I'm about to meet the customer with Glad—I mean, with Mrs. Amelia Gladstone." She smiled and nodded to Cousins III as he reached her. "Another booking? Oh, for a paranormal investigation show? Yeah, great, can you just look up who hasn't had a job in the longest? They probably won't care much about specifics, so let's play fair. Mm-hmm. Thanks, bye."

She hung up. "Sorry about that. My, uh, receptionist. Allow me to introduce—" With this, Mrs. Amelia Gladstone suddenly manifested in full force. Cousins III jumped clear off the ground, which Midi had never seen anyone do before. "This is Mrs. Amelia Gladstone. Mrs. Amelia Gladstone, this is our customer, Cousins Warwick Smith III, the grandson of your…roommate for the next six months." Midi glanced at her customer; Cousins III was holding very still, with eyes very wide, and not speaking. Mrs. Amelia Gladstone was looking prim. "Ah, this is Mrs. Amelia Gladstone's natural appearance. But for your grandfather…" On cue, the ghost shifted her face and clothing and became the old lady from Cousins III's photographs.

Cousins III blanched. "N-Nana?"

Mrs. Amelia Gladstone frowned. "I am not your grandmother, child. However, I suppose your dismay ought to be regarded as a compliment."

Cousins III recovered himself at the words. "I'm sorry, I was thrown for a moment. You certainly don't sound like her."

"Which is why she won't be speaking to your grandfather," Midi cut in. "As we discussed."

"No, of course, that's perfectly fine. As long as he can see her sometimes, I think he'll feel a lot better. He's just finding it hard to adjust to the loneliness, I guess, and I can't visit every day, so…" Cousins III checked himself. "I'm sorry, that's not really important. Um, shall we go in?"

"Right," Midi began, "this is where I leave you. Mrs. Amelia Gladstone will accompany you invisibly for the visit, because of course your grandfather shouldn't know that she's coming in with you. Try to point out the specific locations she'll need to haunt, without letting your grandfather hear you speaking to her. She'll ask you any questions she may have; you'll be able to hear her. If she can't find an opportunity to ask without your grandfather overhearing, she'll come out with you after your visit and ask. Otherwise, she'll just stay there. After the first week, she'll report to me and I'll pass along the word and tell you how it's going, and you can tell me if your grandfather's experience with the haunting is satisfactory. Good?"

"You're not coming in?" Cousins III asked, a little downcast.

Midi blinked at him. "Um, I'm *not* invisible. How would you explain me to your grandfather?"

"Oh. Right." Cousins III looked a little more downcast.

Midi offered, "I can wait around, if it won't be too long and you have more questions."

Cousins III brightened somewhat. "Oh, it'll only be about half an hour. This is a weekday visit."

"All right. I'll see you after your visit."

When Cousins III emerged from his grandfather's house—greatly relieved to be free of the invisible presence of Mrs. Amelia Gladstone—he found Midi on her phone again.

"Well, we can send them Phil if they mainly just want a poltergeist... Yeah. Did you explain to them about separate rental fees if they want an apparition too? ...Okay. Well Phil hasn't had a job in a while and Polly is free anyway, so I'll just go over the options for both of them at the meeting tomorrow and let them decide how much they want to spend for this paranormal investigation show. ...Yup. Okay, thanks, bye."

Cousins III was gripped with ubiquitous curiosity. "Someone is renting ghosts for a TV show? Do all the ghost-hunting shows do that?"

"Oh, it's not the show that's renting the ghosts. It's the people who own the house. They called the ghost-hunting show to come out, but they don't actually have a haunted house. They're trying to get one started. I think they're investing in ghosts for the show so they can run the place as a haunted B&B later." She shrugged. "Some places probably have their own ghosts already. Sometimes people rent them. I dunno, I don't really watch those shows."

"Huh." Cousins III nodded. "What was that about the difference between an apparition and a poltergeist? Oh," he broke off and indicated his car. "Can I give you a ride home, or wherever you're going?" As far as he could tell, Midi had walked from wherever it was she came from.

"You don't mind?"

"No, please."

"All right, thanks! Downtown would be awesome." She followed him to the car.

"Ah, so yes, about apparitions and poltergeists?"

"Well, you rented an apparition, and you've heard of poltergeists, right?"

"I've heard of something like that in movies..."

Midi, folded up on the seat and knees on the dash, said, "I dunno what they do in movies, but basically they don't really have a visible form, but they are considerably better than apparitions at interacting with this plane. By that I mean they can throw stuff. Make knocking noises, turn on your gas stove and blow your house up, things like that."

"…They can?"

"Well, they only *would* if they were spoiled by a grudge. I haven't got any spoiled poltergeists, so don't worry. Mine just slam doors, things like that. Paranormal investigation shows dig that kinda thing, but sometimes they want to actually see a ghost. That's why they might want to rent an apparition too."

"Don't they always want to see the ghosts?"

Midi shrugged. "Like I said, I don't watch those shows. But I think they don't want to see too much too often. People wouldn't believe it." She dug out her phone and poked at something on it. "Maybe they'll want some light orbs to start with…"

Cousins III struggled within himself for two blocks and a stop light. Today, Midi had pink streaks in her hair, purple mascara, enormously baggy camo pants, and a baby blue sweater coated in sequins—he observed this in glances, only mostly when stopped at the light. Then he struggled a little more, and finally collapsed under the weight of unbearable curiosity.

"Light orbs?"

"What?" Midi glanced up at him, baffled.

"You mentioned light orbs. What are those? Not ghosts?"

"Oh, they're ghosts…or at least they're something spiritual. You know, from *that* plane. As far as I can tell they don't have consciousness. They never respond when I talk to them. But they can be, mm, *controlled* isn't quite the word. *Trained*, maybe. If you ever want to rent any, I need access to the haunting location about twenty-four hours in advance, so I can get them placed properly and make sure they are cued to react."

"I think one ghost was all I needed," Cousins III said quickly.

"Okay!" Midi smiled and went back to tapping at her phone.

After a while: "Where to, downtown?"

Glancing up, Midi pointed, "If you turn here and then take a left on Fourth, I'll show you where you can let me off." Cousins III obeyed, scanning the area as he drove—still somewhat in the power of his own curiosity. This was not at all a residential area.

"There, see? Lao's Noodles."

As he pulled over, Cousins III had one last go at stifling his curiosity. *Listen,* he told it, *there's no reason for you to know about where she lives. You barely even know where your own landlord lives. When you rent a car on a business trip, you don't wonder where the Enterprise Rent-A-Car employees live. She's just someone you got a rental from. It's not...*

Midi unbelted and popped the door open.

"You live at a noodle restaurant?"

Cousins III felt a little annoyed with his curiosity for speaking without permission.

Sticking her head back in the door, Midi blinked at him. "No? Just picking up dinner on my way home. I can walk from here, it's not far, thanks for the ride!" She turned away, then back again quickly, "Oh! Uh, we'll be in touch next week, as described, about how your rental is doing. Thanks for your business!"

With the muffled thud of a well-made, expensive car door slamming, she was gone. Cousins III was left alone in his very factory-standard, unadorned Lexus, with nothing to do but go back to his quiet condo and check emails and prepare for his ordinary day at work tomorrow.

Midi stood at the pickup counter, humming cheerfully. Mrs. Amelia Gladstone was rented long-term, and she even got a ride home and didn't have to wait for the bus. Today was a day worthy of an extra-large bowl of ramen.

Throughout the sunset and nightfall, Chester drifted vaguely above the counter where the phone was, gazing off into nothing, waiting. The phone did not ring.

3

During the daily half hour of TV, every dead thing in the strip mall was in the back office of the empty store, watching. During the other twenty-three-and-a-half hours of the day, the activities were miscellaneous. The children attempted to play with anything they could, but Chester kept a mean guard on the phone, and no one allowed them near the TV, for fear that their leeching would be discovered if the children turned it on beyond the present limit. As Jemmie and Polly were not poltergeists, they couldn't interact with much on the physical plane, unless it was electric—and none of the lights were wired up.

When they could, they snuck over to the bookstore and played with turning lights off and on. The old proprietor usually didn't notice, except when they killed his reading light. Then he fiddled with it, failed to get it to turn back on, and promptly lit an oil lamp. When the children, bored and disappointed, abandoned their game and his light came back on, he blew out the lamp and continued reading.

Lord Watley stood in front of the dingy old mirror, manifesting himself with utmost concentration so that his reflection was as clear as possible. This done, he began a meticulous combing and shaping of his large, curling moustache.

In death, Lord Watley had nowhere in particular to be, so he was able to spend any number of hours in this pursuit. He was no longer bound to a short half-hour, as he had been in life. When at last there was nothing more to be done, Lord Watley stood back and gazed with satisfaction at his spectral style.

At just this moment, Jemmie burst through the mirror, shrieking, chased a moment later by Polly. If the two children saw anyone or anything in front of them, they did not bother to evade. They charged straight through Lord Watley's startled and dignified face and carried on, vanishing through the next wall a moment later. Lord Watley, bewildered, shook himself back into shape. Then his spectral gaze landed upon his reflection, and he gave a ghostly moan of dismay at the state of his moustache.

"Oh, my sainted aunt…!"

"Your whatted what, dude?"

The skinny teenager half-appeared from the ceiling. Lord Watley gesticulated vaguely, overcome by his tragedy. The skinny teenager made nothing of this.

"Mrs. Aggy!" he shouted; then, in lower tones, "Oh wait, that's right, she's gone. Uh, *Chester!* Lord Whatsit is totally buggin out, dude!"

A spectral voice drifted from the front of the empty store, "What do you want *me* to do about it?"

Lord Watley sagged as though collapsing into a chair. As there was no chair, he simply floated in a recumbent position and fanned himself with a limp hand. The skinny teenager studied him, then shrugged. "Call somebody?"

A pause, and then Chester's head popped through the wall and he gave the pair a look. "Oh, great idea Bobby—I'll just call an ambulance, shall I?"

"Or, like, the boss, maybe?"

"And what can *she* do?"

"I dunno. I just thought how she doesn't want us getting too upset."

Chester glanced at Lord Watley. "He's just in temporary hysterics. It won't kill him." This being said, Chester vanished.

Bobby, unfazed by the lack of support, lingered nearby, watching Lord Watley progress through his attack of the vapors. However, as Chester had noticed, the event would not, after all, kill him. Eventually, Lord Watley was forced to come back to death. With quavering limbs, he pushed against nothing, regained standing posture, and once again faced the mirror.

"Ohhhh," he moaned, "the unmitigated horror!"

Bobby mouthed the words in awe, clearly thinking they were some kind of strange foreign tongue, or possibly a magical incantation. The eccentricities of old ghosts always impressed him.

Lord Watley gravely began again with his toilette.

Bobby promptly and completely lost interest and left.

Chester returned to balefully glare at the phone, which did not ring.

The owners of The Barton House did not rent an apparition in addition to their poltergeist, but Midi did successfully manage to sell them on the idea of a couple spirit orbs. They were definitely considering an apparition for the future, though—possibly if they could get the paranormal investigation show to come back again in the fall, it would get the best ratings during the Halloween season. The main problem was that so far, they hadn't yet sorted out their entire story for the haunted B&B, so they weren't sure what type of apparition they wanted for their haunting.

"No worries, we can work with practically any story," Midi assured them. "Just as a heads-up, though, if you want to rent an apparition in October, you'll need to figure out which type by early September, at the latest, and reserve your rental. My apparitions tend to all be booked pretty solid in October."

"Okay, we'll keep that in mind." The owner turned to her partner. "We'll work on the show-runners when they come this time and try to pin them down as early as possible. Scheduling will be the main issue. We can worry about the ghost story over the summer."

"I still say little girl ghost. Nothing creepier than a little girl ghost."

"Old-ladies-way-worse," the owner shot back, under her breath.

Midi smiled brightly. "No matter what, Acme Rent-a-Ghost has you covered!"

The owners of The Barton House Haunted Bed and Breakfast seemed powerfully convinced by this classic sales line. They signed their rental agreement with no fuss.

Two days later, Midi kept an appointment at The Barton House to look over the property and let the owners tell her where they wanted the paranormal activity to happen. And the week after that, shortly before the TV crew showed up, Midi brought Phil and explained these details to him. She also brought the spirit orbs and spent the hour of dusk training them into their proper locations and teaching them the correct triggers to light them up. Her smaller spirit orb was a little slow to learn verbal cues, but it wasn't a significant problem. It just took a little longer before Midi was confident they would function properly the next day.

It was nighttime when Midi wrapped up and left. She had brought her scooter, because The Barton House was a little too far off the bus route. It had been a warm day, for March, but that had gone with the sunset, and now Midi was regretting that she only had her DraculaPants hoodie. Sadly, her pineapple-print leggings were also a little on the thin side. They certainly didn't keep the wind off. She wished she'd worn her electric orange jumpsuit.

Alas, there was nothing for it but to get through the drive as quickly as possible. She put a mask on to protect her nose and lips a little bit from the wind, and made her scooter do top speed, a blazing 30 mph, all the way to Lao's—except when stopped at intersections.

Lao's Noodles was brightly lit and always too hot, because only one of the exhaust fans in the kitchen worked, and that none too well. To Midi, it was like stepping into paradise, and she sighed and promptly began to thaw.

Before she could even get to the counter, however, a fellow who had been sitting alone at one of the tiny tables suddenly stood, facing her, and raised a hand with an awkward, "Oh, um…hello."

Midi blinked at him for a minute, struggling to place him. He was so exactly like practically everyone that she wasn't even sure, for a moment, if she actually thought he looked familiar. "Hi!" she said, still drawing a blank.

"The, um, I mean, Mrs. Amelia Gladstone is doing quite well," he said, and Midi's brain flashed to life.

"Ah! Cousins Something-Something number Three!"

Cousins III's heart panged a bit with chagrin. One could easily tell, with a reaction like that, that one had not been recognized. Even if one had recognized Midi despite the kitty-cat-face mask she had on—or perhaps partly because of it. Cousins III was not-quite-so bothered that she hadn't remembered most of his name. She got the vital bits, at least.

"Yes, ah, would you like to—" Midi had already dropped into the seat opposite him. Cousins III said "um" and sat back down himself.

"I sure hope Gladstone will stay with your grandfather for ages and ages," Midi was already saying. "Long life to him! *Ya! Lao-ba!*" This last, over her shoulder. Cousins III startled slightly, but bore the sudden shouting with philosophical patience.

"Jjajangmeon?" the lady behind the counter shouted back.

"Yes please!" Midi tucked her mask into her hoodie pocket and rubbed her hands together. "Not that we don't like her, of course," she continued conversationally. "But she can be a bit of a strain on the others, the way she is."

"She?" Cousins III glanced over at the lady behind the counter, then belatedly rediscovered the trail the conversation was apparently still on. "Oh! Mrs. Gladstone.

Yes, I can see that." He poked a portion of the noodle dish in front of him. "She's doing quite well."

"You said," Midi agreed, agreeably. "You said that two days ago on the phone, too. You like the jjamppong?" She pointed at his bowl.

Cousins III hesitated to make a definitive call. "It's very spicy," he said. The owner brought Midi her own plate and set it down. Cousins III blinked at the pile of black-sauce noodles; it did not look appetizing to him. He began to look more kindly upon his own food. He found the spice level difficult, but not beyond him. He thought, on the whole, that he would triumph in the end, if he continued slowly and rested at intervals.

Then Midi up-ended a condiment bottle over her noodles and Cousins III blanched a bit and couldn't help but ask, "Is that…mayonnaise?"

"Mm-hmm." She mixed the now-far-less-appetizing noodles around and asked, "Hey, what's your job?"

"Eh?"

"What do you do for a living? You're rich, right?"

"Oh. I'm the Vice President of product development at ZyTech Industries."

Midi blinked at him, chewing, then swallowed and said, "I don't know what that means and it sounds really boring."

Cousins III let this sink in for a moment. Then he said, "It is."

"But it pays a lot?"

"It does pay a lot."

A sage nod, accompanied by further chewing. Then: "So why are you eating here?"

"I beg your pardon?" Cousins III had heard her just fine. He just didn't have a ready answer for that. Not one he wanted to admit to, anyway.

"I mean, the noodles here are good, but it's cheap food. I guess if you want noodles, there are fancier places. You know, with bigger chairs and tables and stuff." She pointed to the street. "Usually don't see many Lexuses parked in front of this place."

It was a canny observation, and Cousins III struggled mightily in his mind. He had a tragic tendency toward honesty, but he just didn't think now was the time. "I was…curious," he admitted, finally. That covered the facts, technically.

Midi obviously didn't care to delve any further into the subject; she was busy delving into her noodles. Cousins III gave a part of his attention to his own food for a moment, but he didn't keep it there for very long.

"How many ghosts do you have?" he asked suddenly.

"How many?" Midi echoed around a mouthful of noodles. Cousins III nodded as she swallowed. "Oof, I have no idea. Counting the poltergeists and orbs and all?"

"Do they count for a lot?"

"I guess. I never counted the orbs, just keep them all in storage, basically. There are plenty of poltergeists—enough I've never had to turn anyone down who wanted one. I tend to rent out all the apparitions in October, so maybe…twenty of those, all told? I don't know, really, I'd have to ask Chester."

"Who is Chester?" Cousins III asked, momentarily irritated.

"Receptionist," Midi answered, without noticing.

"Oh." Cousins III thought that he might have perhaps heard this name when he first called, but he wasn't sure. "So he's not a friend?"

"Friend?" Midi hummed. "Maybe a little bit? He's a ghost, though."

"*Oh.*" Cousins III was mollified, for reasons unsuspected by Midi—and unadmitted by himself. Then, in a less emotionally fraught frame of mind, he mused, "I was talking to a ghost on the phone."

Midi found this to be a statement of fact that required no response from her—or if it did, her noodles required her more. She did not ponder how Cousins III felt about this detail. Cousins III, for his part, sat there wondering how he might go about getting one of his developers to research ghosts' interactions with electronics, with an eye to expanding the communications field in that direction.

However, before Cousins III quite expected it, Midi had finished her noodles and was leaning back with a sigh—though not far back, as the small chairs were not stable enough to allow such acrobatics. "Well, it was nice running into you," she said, unzipping her fanny pack and digging out some money. The lady from behind the counter suddenly manifested at their table to clear away and accept payment. Cousins III hadn't seen her approach, and for a moment was half-sure she was another ghost.

Then Cousins III realized she was going to leave just like that, and he stammered, "Can I offer you a ride home?"

Midi gave him a funny, half-laughing look. "Ride? Thanks, but the way the streets are, it's quicker to walk. And I've got my scooter anyway."

Still in the tyrannical grip of his curiosity, Cousins III persisted, "M-May I walk you home, then?"

But Midi, who failed to notice the slight drop in his timbre, was already on her feet and going. Her only response was, "Why would you do that?" followed by a wave over the shoulder and "Thanks again for your business, enjoy your dinner!" Then she was gone.

Cousins III was already standing, and now he took the first step to following her, but he was arrested by a sudden iron grip on his arm. Turning, he saw the owner, who smiled broadly at him and held out an open palm.

Midi vanished as Cousins III paid for his meal. The owner took his money and pointed to his bowl with a questioning look. "I'll...take it to go," he said, resigned to the ultimate futility of human existence. *'Meaningless, meaningless!' says the Teacher,* he thought to himself, as he accepted his little plastic bag with the Styrofoam container full of distilled lava masquerading as food.

Midi cheerfully braved the final stretch of cold, fortified with the bountiful heat from the noodle shop.

At the empty strip mall store, the phone rang. Chester heard it, but they were presently right in the middle of the daily half hour of TV vouchsafed to the ghosts, and Chester did not go and answer it. He had heard that the king or whatever now required employers to give their employees a lunch break. Chester figured that since he monitored the phone 23.5 hours per day, he could take a half-hour lunch at 7:30 p.m. if he wished.

"What if that was your big break, dude?"

Chester did not take his eyes from the TV. "I have no idea what you just said," he announced flatly. Overall, Chester felt he had done quite well in keeping up with the times and learning to speak the new English, but Bobby was a very new ghost and tended to defeat him. This did not trouble Chester, however. He mostly considered it Bobby's fault.

"What if it was gonna be a job for you this time?"

Chester still did not look away from the TV.

"It isn't."

Two customers in March was pretty good. March wasn't a hot season for ghost rentals. October was the holiday rush in Midi's business, of course, and beyond that the summer months were usually somewhat busy. A ghost at summer camp was a classic. Midi had to charge more in summer to cover the cost of travel outside the city, delivering her ghosts. And then there was a market for ghosts at Christmas, thanks always to Mr. Charles Dickens, so generally speaking Midi had enough to live on from June to December. But January through May were her lean months. Any rentals she got tended to be oddball contracts—first-time customers with their own unique, personal reasons for renting a ghost, and not likely to be in the specter market again any time soon.

Having a long-term rental out on contract was helpful—it gave Midi at least some assurance of an income for the next few months. Of course, Mr. Cousins Warwick Smith, Sr. could still die at any time, and then Mrs. Amelia Gladstone would lose her client. The rental term was six months, but the early termination fee was set low due to the ephemeral nature of life, particularly where elderly men were concerned.

The electronic doorbell buzzed, and Midi glanced up as Mrs. Amelia Gladstone drifted in. Some ghosts reported over the phone, but Mrs. Amelia Gladstone had not deigned to learn the use of electricity yet. She called in person to report, even though there was nothing really to say—except that all was going well—and her host could not offer her tea. Mrs. Amelia Gladstone always felt ever so slightly dissatisfied about this. Midi might call it "reporting," but to her it was in the guise of a social call, and there was something distressingly incomplete about the whole process without a cup of tea.

Still, with her iron determination to uphold her duties, Mrs. Amelia Gladstone made her regular reports punctually, sitting perfectly erect, and she endured the lack of a cup of tea with a fortitude that would have conquered all the tortures the best Inquisitor could invent.

"Job's still good? Okay."

Mrs. Amelia Gladstone felt a pang at the brevity in the living girl's response. Humans these days simply knew nothing of decorum.

"And how are you? Energy levels not getting depleted by playing Mrs. Smith all the time? And how's the house? Okay?"

With the appearance of a deep breath, Mrs. Amelia Gladstone said, "One question at a time, please. My energy is fine, thank you for asking. My constitution is quite good. And the house is…sufficient. I cannot speak for the décor, but a widower cannot be relied upon for such things."

Midi nodded. "Mmm." Then, narrowing her eyes: "And how's the grandpa doing? Healthy?"

Mrs. Amelia Gladstone found this to be in poor taste. It would have been one thing if he had really been her husband, and if the question had been phrased better, such as: "And I do hope Mr. Smith's health is keeping up in spite of this wet weather?" With things as they were, the inquiry was simply a financial one, and it felt decidedly low-class to speak so brazenly of money.

She again summoned her fortitude. "As far as I can see, Mr. Smith, Sr.'s melancholy has lifted considerably. He had something of a head cold when I first arrived. That seems to have cleared. Perhaps the matters are related." Mrs. Amelia Gladstone rose from her sitting position—which she maintained with perfect posture, despite having nothing in Midi's apartment that could serve as a decent chair—and began to button her gloves back on. "Now if you will excuse me, I must return before dusk. It is inconvenient to conceal myself from second-sighted people once evening falls."

"All right, thanks for the update! I'll let the grandson know."

Pausing on the threshold, with only her furthest left side cut off by being inside and through the closed door, Mrs. Amelia Gladstone replied, "Mr. Smith, Sr.'s grandson has been to see him and has observed his grandfather's progress for himself. I have also already informed young Mr. Smith the Third of everything I have reported to you today."

"Did you? Cool, thanks!"

Mrs. Amelia Gladstone paused for only a moment. In the end, she bowed slightly, turned, and left through the closed door without another word. She had contemplated, for that moment, whether she ought to inform Midi of the further questions Mr. Smith the younger had asked her—for not all of his solicitude had been for his own grandfather. However, in the end, she decided that Mr. Smith the younger had not asked anything untoward, and perhaps he had simply been attempting to make conversation.

He had done it poorly, if that were the case, but judging by his grandfather, eloquence did not run in that family.

4

On a fine day in April, Chester drifted about the roof of the desolate end of the strip mall.

He had begun by arranging himself in a sitting position on the edge of the roof, but maintaining postures with reference to solid objects took some concentration, because the solid objects, after all, did not lend him any help. He went from sitting to lying down to simply drifting. Some of him was out in the sunlight—at least his head always was—and some of him was inside the roof or walls of the building at various times. The only thing Chester maintained was his unimpeded view, because he was watching the coming of spring.

He was doing so unobserved, because it was daytime, and the dim luster of a ghost's energy was invisible in the sunlight—except perhaps to those with unusually keen spiritual perception. Since the main traffic at this strip mall was down at the dollar store at the other end of the parking lot, Chester felt little fear of being spotted. He studied the parking lot with considerable interest. It was nice to see some of the stronger weeds returning to resume their dissection of the asphalt. Chester was particularly fond of that patch of thistles in the handicap parking spot…

The phone rang.

Chester's mildly pleased expression darkened. He steeled himself, then descended through the roof much as a man ascends the scaffold—same attitude, opposite direction. Finally, he paused in front of the rotary telephone, which was jangling away. "Chesser! Phoooooone!" came Jemmie's call from somewhere out of sight.

"I know!" he shouted back, then turned to give the thing one final glare of recrimination. At last, with a sigh, he stuck his head into it. "Acme Rent-a-Ghost, specters, poltergeists, and astral bodies, this is Chester, how may I help you?"

A throat-clearing sound. "Hello, again. I called the other day to ask about the types of poltergeist activity you offer…"

Inside the telephone, Chester's eye twitched.

"Yes, hello. What can I help you with today? Did you decide to rent a poltergeist?"

"Um, no, today I was wondering if you offer any sort of group discount for large orders of spirit orbs?"

Chester's ethereal teeth clicked together—at least, they didn't click, because they weren't solid, but they became more tightly aligned. He spoke through them: "How many spirit orbs are you asking about?"

"However many would be discounted."

Chester's chest seemed to rise and fall heavily. "I can't say, sir. The largest order of spirit orbs we ever filled at one time was ten. I believe the boss charged no fee for the tenth one, so it was something like 'rent nine get one free' if that counts."

"Oh, she did? Is that how she does it normally?"

"That was a single occasion. Usually our rates are defined and adhered to. May I ask why you need so many spirit orbs?"

"Oh, no reason. I was just wondering if you had a bulk rate or discount on them. Offering special rates can encourage people to spend a little more than they had planned to."

Chester's tight smile was still invisible inside the telephone, though it was beginning to be audible in his voice.

"Very true, sir, but as I said, we haven't had any customers who needed spirit orbs in such a high quantity. The usual number is two or three per location. Will there be anything else today?"

"I see. So you said before that your boss visits the location to place the spirit orbs, right?"

"I did say that before. I said several times that she always personally brings all rented ghosts to the location because we can't carry maps. You may recall."

"Right…so how long does she stay when she has to place the spirit orbs? It's longer than with apparitions, right?"

The line became slightly static-y for a moment as Chester balled his pudgy vaporous hands into pudgy vaporous fists. "That depends, sir. Some apparitions need a detailed tour of their haunting ground, though it's true that they usually can just be dropped off and quickly introduced. Spirit orbs need to be trained, which can take up to a few hours, but usually they pick it up very quickly. They aren't very complicated overall."

"So she stays a couple hours to train the spirit orbs…" This, Chester did not respond to, because it was muttered as though the caller was not speaking to him. Then, more definitely directed at Chester: "Is that a couple hours per orb or for the whole bunch?"

"A couple hours for all of them, sir. But again, 'all of them' is usually only a few. If you are planning a large order of spirit orbs, perhaps exceeding ten, the boss might need to arrive the night before they are needed so she has plenty of time to get them all placed and trained."

"Would she stay the whole night?" The caller did little to conceal his audible delight and hope.

Chester felt a black impatience beginning to creep into his ethereal essence. "She will if it's necessary for her to get the job done. Did you want to rent some spirit orbs or not?"

"I don't know. So she can be out all night for work…and she's not leaving anyone at home who would be, um, bothered by that?"

Chester had a crick in his essence by now. "As I told you before, sir, I can't discuss my employer's personal life with you. If you want to talk to *her*, you should call her directly. I believe you have her phone number."

"Oh no, I was just saying. I'll get back to you about the orbs!"

Click.

Chester withdrew his head from the telephone and rubbed his neck. "Try it next time and I'll—" he hissed.

"Ooh." Turning, he saw Jemmie and Polly. "Chesser...your eyes is lookin a little dark."

"There's black in them!"

Blinking rapidly, Chester shook himself. "I'm all right, it's nothing. Just an annoying caller."

"You gotsa be careful 'bout that, you know."

Jemmie nodded his sage agreement. "Be careful!"

"I'm fine, really. It's only a human, anyway." With that, Chester rose through the ceiling and resumed his enjoyment of the spring day as best he could.

Jemmie turned to Polly and gave her a brotherly lecture: "Now, remember what Midi says about gettin angry?"

"Turnin black—turn back. Keepin clear—no fear!"

"That's right. Low look here and show me your eyes..."

Polly widened them beyond corporeal limits.

"Good—all clear! Now check mine."

Jemmie did the same, and Polly announced, "Clear!"

"Good. Let's go play!"

5

June hit like July that year. The ghosts didn't know this, of course, until Midi showed up three weeks earlier than usual. They couldn't feel heat or cold, rain or snow or sun. But they could see, and when Midi climbed into the back room through the loading dock, they could see the sweat putting dark spots on her yellow tank top, and the loose strands of black hair sticking to her neck.

"Ahhhhhh!" Midi threw her head back and her arms wide. "Finally!"

"I say," Lord Watley began, but Bobby interrupted.

"Must be blisterin."

Midi turned and pulled the shutter back down over the docking bay door. It wasn't a big dock; it wouldn't accommodate big trucks. It was made just big enough for a forklift to slide a pallet through, or possibly for people on a pickup truck's bed to hand things through. Midi had the key to the shutter's padlock. A stack of decaying pallets outside hid a small section of the rear wall, and that was where Midi typically left her scooter. Her presence at the strip mall left no trace for an observer to detect.

"I was debating sticking it out at the apartment a little longer, but the forecast says it'll be like this or worse for at least a week. If it goes back down to reasonable for late June, maybe I'll get out of your hair again for a bit, but right now I just couldn't take any more of that place." She dusted her hands off on her Mickey Mouse shorts and bent to unlace her combat boots.

The ghosts that had not already been in the back room had heard her arrival and begun to drift in. Chester appeared, and immediately his soft face spread out in a broad smile.

"Oh but I say, my dear girl, quite fond and all, but this is terribly shocking."

Midi barely looked at him. "Yes, all right, carry on Lord Watley. You'll get over it in a bit; you do every year." She looked around. "Where are the ladies?" Midi usually did not subdivide the erstwhile women in her employ, but simply called all of them *the ladies*.

"Shopping," Bobby answered, rolling his eyes.

"What, all of them?"

"If it's daylight and they can't be seen," Chester explained, "then yes, pretty much all of them, all the time." The ladies all loved to investigate stores of all kinds. Individually, they came from many eras and walks of life, but whether maiden, matron, or crone, they all liked to go shopping together during the day, and they often talked together all night. "You're going to handle the telephone while you're here, right?" Chester's smile widened just a little further.

"If you like. Where are the kids?"

"Midi!" two voices shrieked, and two small streaks of dim light came through one wall and charged her. They passed through her without hitch and turned and came back.

Midi sighed and spread her arms again. "I'll give you a week to cut that out," she said. The children entertained themselves by running through her, back and forth, while Midi asked the assembly, "So do we still have running water, or did the company finally realize it wasn't shut off?"

"I don't know, we haven't checked lately. We didn't know you were coming so soon."

"No worries, I'll check it."

"Nah, I got it," Bobby said quickly. "You chill. I'll ask Phil or one of them to check it."

"Aw, thanks!" Midi went over to the couch and dragged off the old sheet that served as a dust cover. She flopped down. "Man, it's so nice in here with you guys," she sighed. "I might even bring a blanket and some long PJs from home."

"Midi, Midi, Midi!" Polly bounced through the couch. "Can you play the little TV?"

"Right now?" She smiled. "I guess. It's fully charged. Remember, you can't touch this one, okay? You'll drain the battery." She pulled out her phone and started streaming a show for them. "How long do you run the TV now?" she asked the others.

"Forty minutes," Chester answered. Midi nodded.

"Okay, good. I'll have to re-run my calculations." Midi had a microwave, a kettle, a little-used lamp, a nearly-never-used fan, and her phone charger. Apart from the charger, she kept these things in the strip mall, for summers. The ghosts would need to give up their TV so that she could use the electricity instead, but as a trade-off, Midi played stuff on her phone for them. And all summer long, wherever she went for meetings with customers, she'd charge her phone on anyone and everyone else's dime, just to keep from needing to do it at the strip mall.

A rumbling sound reached them from the bathroom, and Bobby appeared a moment later. "Water's still running! Told Phil to run the rust out and then shut it off."

"Thanks!"

"Yeah dude."

Midi began unpacking her little backpack of necessities. Her living area hadn't been touched since the summer before—the spectral residents couldn't disturb her things, and the poltergeists were all careful not to. So everything was very much as she'd left it. Midi had microwave ramen for dinner. Chester watched her wistfully. And then the phone rang.

Chester beamed. "Midi…telephone."

"Oh, right." She hopped up and scampered up to the storefront room, muttering, "I gotta get a longer wire and bring it back here…"

As it was, the telephone's curly cord was more than long enough to stretch, so as long as it wasn't a wrong number, she'd be back on the couch in a minute anyway, but her idea this year was to set up a little end table so she wouldn't need to get up anymore.

Picking up the receiver, Midi said, "Hello, Acme Rent-a-Ghost, specters, poltergeists, and astral bodies, this is Midi, how may I help you?"

A short silence. Then: "What?"

Midi looked at the telephone with a funny expression. "Acme Rent-a-Ghost. Can I help you?"

"…Midi?"

"Yes?"

"Oh."

A long pause.

"Yes? Who is this?"

"I didn't realize you answered this number. You never did before. It was always the receptionist. Did something happen to him?"

"He's fine, who is this?"

"Oh. This is Cousins Warwick Smith III."

"Ah, Cousins number Three! Gladstone's customer! Is everything all right with her and your grandfather?"

Saying this, Midi had returned to the back room as planned, and the ghosts heard her. As she flopped back onto the couch, Chester caught her eye. He was doing some oddish things with his ghostly eyebrows and pointing to the receiver. Midi frowned at him, unable to read his Afterlife Sign Language.

Cousins III was reporting something in the affirmative as Chester attempted to communicate quietly. Midi shook her head, then shrugged, then finally mouthed, *What?*

Chester whispered, "He's been calling, lately." Midi pointed to the receiver and raised her eyebrows. Chester nodded. Midi frowned again and pointed from Chester to herself, back and forth repeatedly. He shook his head. "I didn't call you because he hasn't rented anything. He just calls to ask about things."

Finally, Midi clapped a hand over the receiver. "What things?" she whispered.

Chester gave her a look and made it short. He pointed at her.

Midi continued clueless and pointed at herself, eyebrows once again climbing the heights.

"You," Chester whispered, nodding.

"Great, so glad to hear that," Midi said aloud into the phone, then covered the receiver again. "What about me?" she whispered.

But that was not something that could be readily abbreviated, so Chester just shrugged and rolled his eyes.

It seemed Cousins III had run out of things to say about Mrs. Amelia Gladstone, and now was falling unfortunately silent, so Midi prompted: "So were you interested in another rental, then? Is that why you called the office?"

Cousins III said, "Um."

Hitherto, Cousins III had been able to find plenty of excuses to call the Rent-a-Ghost office. He had questions, so many questions, and even if most of them weren't directly about the ghost rental service, he had those too and could always produce one. He had never bothered to write down a list of his questions because he had never been in any kind of difficulty when it came to remembering them.

Just now, he wished very much that he had at least jotted a note about the question he planned to ask today. But he had expected the receptionist to answer, and he had never experienced a blanked out memory while talking to the receptionist; alas for a lack of prescience.

In short: because Midi had answered the phone, Cousins III had sadly suffered a sudden evaporation of all thoughts in his head. He could not come up with a question.

Not one he dared ask, anyway.

"Polly, remember, don't touch the phone—I mean the little TV!" Midi's voice dropped back to a normal tone. "Sorry about that. You were about to say?"

"Are you…babysitting?"

A snort. "Oh no, Polly is a little girl ghost. They're watching a show on my phone."

Cousins III's curiosity surged belatedly to life and came to his rescue. "Why can't they touch it?"

"It's got a battery. They'll drain it. Especially a lithium-ion battery, those go down quick in contact with ghosts."

"Oh. So they can't touch electronics? They would ruin them?"

"No, no. *Batteries*. Electronics that plug in are fine. In fact, just about the only things they *can* interact with are power sources, electric things and all that. If it's plugged in, they can touch things and affect the power in them, turn them on and off, control them a bit. In fact, if a customer is really tight in the budget, sometimes I rent them an apparition who can also do poltergeist stuff, it's just they're limited to electric things. No slamming doors, throwing books, that stuff. See?"

"I think so." Cousins III processed all this. Midi had a way of speaking that sometimes came at him out of left field. "So apparitions can interact with anything that uses electricity, much as poltergeists can interact with matter. But they drain batteries if they touch them?"

"That's what I said." Midi was patient, if slightly baffled by the sudden game of "echo."

"So…this being the office line, which usually your receptionist answers, I take it you're not speaking on a mobile phone right now?"

"Right. It's one of those old spinners."

"Spinners?"

"You know, with the piece that spins around over the numbers."

"Oh, a rotary phone!"

"Sure, that."

There was a short silence while Midi waited for Cousins III to come to his point, and Cousins III tried to find a point to come to.

"So you are presently at your office?"

"Uh-huh."

"Where is that?"

Midi glanced around. "Um. Why?"

"I just wondered where the Rent-a-Ghost office is."

Midi hummed, twisting the cord around her fingers. "Somewhere cheap."

"Cheap?"

"Practically free," she said, grinning.

"Are you there often?"

"At the office? Not at all, usually. But it's summer now so I'll be living here for a while."

"You'll live at your office? Why?"

"Free air conditioning!" Midi answered. Her tone was exactly as it would have been if she had won the lottery.

Chester observed this pointless conversation with a sardonic smile. Midi seemed to have forgotten that there was supposed to be a reason for a customer to call her rental office.

Cousins III apparently asked what she meant, and Midi began to explain. Bobby watched the streaming show with the children, Lord Watley began to come out of his impropriety fit, and the rumble of running water shut off. Chester drifted up through the roof and resumed his contemplation of parking lot weeds. Last year, some loitering teenagers had taken to smoking at this edge of the lot, and one of them had been fond of snacking on sunflower seeds. As a consequence, this year there were several large sunflowers coming up through the cracks and along the edge of the lot. They were growing big and strong, though not yet blooming. Chester was anticipating the day their big heads would open up into those giant yellow flowers.

The sun began to set, and it was somewhere in the middle of doing this when the ladies returned. Chester greeted them politely and informed them of Midi's early arrival. However, he didn't go in with them. He remained half-out, watching the sunset, blissfully free of any telephone responsibility for the first time since last September.

At dusk, of course, he had to go in; the dark made him visible, and even though the strip mall was ill-frequented, it wouldn't do any of them any good for someone to spot a ghost sticking out of the empty unit.

In the back room, Chester found the usual evening bustle—a little heightened by the presence of Midi. She was stirring a spoonful of marshmallow fluff into a mug of hot chocolate, while the ladies were doing what they did best: *talking*.

"They're called earbuds," Midi was saying. "See the speakers on the TV? They're like a tiny version of that. They play sound."

"I told you they weren't jewelry!" one lady said to another.

"Then what, pray, are all the colors for?" another lady argued.

"Cuz colors," Midi shrugged. The debate raged on. "Hey Chester," she said, catching sight of him.

"Your telephone call is over," he observed.

"Oh, yeah."

"Did he rent anyone?"

Midi frowned. "Actually, he didn't, come to think of it. Funny. Hey, what was all that stuff you were pantomiming about?"

Chester glanced around the room. Practically all the ghosts were present—except, of course, Gladstone, whose absence was a continual relief. The children were also gone, off playing somewhere, the little TV quiet and dark now. "Oh...nothing," he said.

"You said he called before, though, right? But he didn't rent anyone, and he said everything is fine with Gladstone..."

"Oh, was your caller the boy whose grandfather is keeping company with Amelia?" a lady asked.

"Yeah, Chester says he's called a few times."

"Are we talking about the human boy who harbors a secret passion for Miss Midi?" another lady inquired. General attention was coming around to the topic, drawing all translucent eyes.

"Boy who what's a *what?*" Midi rather yelped, sitting up.

"Dude!"

"Oh, I say!"

"The boy who *fancies* you, my dear. Mr. Smith the younger, I believe," another lady agreed.

"She means he's taken a shine to ya," another lady agreed.

"And well he hath done, truly," another lady agreed, "for so Amelia spake plainly to me, to make a short tale, to wit: that the grandson asketh after thee at every turn and chance, and speaketh of nought else unto her, but of thee, dear."

"…What did she say?" Bobby asked, awed.

"She said, young man, that our young Miss Amelia speaks to that human boy when he visits his grandfather, and the boy talks of nothing but little Miss Midi. To Amelia, his interest is quite plain, as she tells us," explained another lady.

"Quite so," another lady agreed.

Midi had been gawping in a moderately unsuccessful effort to take all this in. At this point, she burst out, "Are you all telling me that Cousins III *likes* me!?"

"They are," Chester said, "and he does."

Midi stared at him.

"That's what I was trying to tell you. He calls all the time just to ask obnoxious questions. He pretends it's about a rental but he always works it around to asking anything he can about *you*. He likes you."

Midi's arm had slackened somewhat, allowing the mug to tip a little more than advisable. She hissed as hot cocoa scalded her through her shirt. A chorus of sympathies from the ladies echoed all around. The more recently deceased among them made abortive movements as though to help, before they remembered that they couldn't and went back to their tutting.

Chester smiled broadly, for he heard the telephone begin to ring.

"Midi," he said, "telephone."

In a flurry of limbs and well-regulated cocoa mug balancing, Midi darted to the front room and answered the phone. She was back a moment later. "Wrong number," she pronounced to the room. The ladies were already continuing the discussion without her, and were not to be interrupted.

"I think he's an excellent prospect. He has a small fortune, you know."

"And he's just a year her senior, which is perfect."

"He hath a kindly nature, by my troth."

"A steady boy like that would be good for little Midi."

"An' kick me if he ain't a handsome feller!"

"What's troth?" Bobby asked.

"All right, enough!" Midi shouted. All transparent eyes turned to her. She huffed, then took a bracing gulp of her cocoa and planted her hands on her hips. "Before you all start planning my wedding, I'm going to go settle this question for myself."

"Oh I say, wot?" Lord Watley fuddled.

Midi straightened up another inch in her heroic pose. "I'm going to find out if he really likes me or if you all got your ethers twisted." Valorously, she stomped over, snatched up her phone—or little TV, as it was known—and tapped at the screen. She held it to her ear and waited. The rest of the room waited breathlessly—as usual.

Two moments later: "Hello? Cousins number Three? This is Midi. Can you meet me at Lao's for dinner?"

Chester cast a mournful eye at her.

"Great. What time? I don't know, what time is it now… In an hour? Sure, in an hour." Midi moved toward the bathroom door, then paused. "About?" She blinked, glanced around the room, and answered, "It's about dinner!" Then she tapped the phone to end call and disappeared into the bathroom to wash up.

6

Cousins III acted expeditiously upon receiving Midi's summons. He left the office and went straight to the noodle shop and waited twenty minutes, removing his suit jacket at once and quickly beginning to regret his long sleeves. He had never rolled up his shirt sleeves before. Only when he began to fear that his deodorant was going to fail him did he finally unbutton the cuffs and fold them up, carefully and neatly.

Two minutes later, Midi arrived. She was wearing a purple romper with a teal striped shirt under it, her hair in pigtail braids so thin and tight they almost stood up on their own. Her shoes were strange things Cousins III had never seen before; later that night when he Googled them he learned they were called *geta*. Midi came with a neon pink backpack, an orange camo fanny pack, sparkly fingernails, multicolored bracelets, and a flower painted on her face. Her top lip was teal and the bottom one was lavender.

Cousins III had not seen her in person in a few months, and he was momentarily deprived of speech. He felt like insanity had walked up and punched him in the face and told him, "She's the prettiest girl you ever saw in your life," and then handed him an ice cream cone by way of apology, leaving him bruised, pleased, and marvelously enlightened respecting certain subjects.

During his moment of catharsis-induced inactivity, Midi approached, already saying, "Whew, I forgot this place is a bad idea in the summer. *Lao-ba!*" And she passed Cousins III by, heading to the counter.

Cousins III gathered himself, gained his feet, and followed. Midi turned at the counter, having just paid, and said, "I got us cold noodles to go. We're better off outside."

"Where outside?" he managed to ask, though to him it seemed like the sidewalk or the surface of Mars were all one and the same to him—and all the very best idea in the world.

"I don't know. The park is a bit of a walk but we can find somewhere."

"I can drive," he offered. "The car is air-conditioned."

"Ah!" Midi beamed at him, pointing a finger at his nose. "I forgot! You're loaded!"

Considering his tax bracket, Cousins III wouldn't have used the term "loaded" to describe himself; but taking things on a comparative basis, he decided not to argue. It was an excellent decision. Midi's multicolored smile had temporarily dislocated the synapses in his brain that handled coherent speech. Any attempt to discuss finance at this point would have come out fairly inarticulate. Cousins III thus proved the proverb: *Even fools are thought wise if they keep silent.*

What followed was that Cousins III waited in his car while Midi ran into another nearby shop and returned with drinks—or something that came in Styrofoam drink cups, at least, he didn't really ask—and then he drove them to the park. Midi plugged her phone into his car charger as soon as she was buckled, and the strange smell of unknown noodles mingled with the familiar clean vinyl smell of car air conditioning for two minutes.

Then: the park.

"This is better," Midi declared, leading the way to an unoccupied picnic table. "It's always much cooler here. Of course, your car is even better, but I don't want to have to worry about spilling anything and leaving a smell you'll never get rid of. Plus I need a table for these." She raised the drink-cups.

"Why?" Cousins III followed in happy mystification.

"For this!"

So saying, Midi set out the cups. Cousins III, entrusted with noodles, slowly withdrew them from their takeaway baggie and removed the lids while he watched. One of the cups proved to be empty; the other two contained a chocolate milkshake and a bright orange slushie, respectively. Popping off both lids, Midi picked these up and poured them together into the empty cup. When it was full of combined brown and orange, she re-lidded the two half-empty cups and pushed them over to Cousins III. "Help yourself."

Cousins III cautiously accepted the half-milkshake and half-slushie as Midi pointed to the two bowls and said two different words that Cousins III didn't understand at all. When he realized she was asking for his preference, he said, "Oh! Um…which do you prefer?"

"I like both."

"Oh." Cousins III considered mysterious foreign noodles for a moment, consulting his extremely limited experience. "Are they spicy?"

"Yeah."

Chagrined: "Ah." Then, with renewed hope: "Which one is…less spicy?"

"That one."

Cousins III humbly accepted the indicated bowl, hoping for the best.

The best did not occur. What terrors of pain must lurk in that other bowl, which Midi shoveled away so gleefully. Still, Cousins III could at least say that whatever he was eating was less spicy than whatever he had eaten last time, and once he adjusted for the burn, it was tasty, in a strange way. He sipped a bit at the chocolate milkshake, which he tended to favor over orange slushie. It killed the burn nicely, but didn't go well with the flavors of the food. He tried the orange slushie. It was better with the taste of the food but didn't do much for the burn.

Cousins III paused, taking a minute to regard the bizarre alien he had fallen for. Then, overcome by the madness of his passion, he dumped the rest of the orange slushie into his chocolate milkshake cup. He was, after all, the distant son of great Norman conquerors, now braving an inexplicable dinner in the park.

As for speech that evening, Midi asked Cousins III a little about his work, but then glazed over when he tried to answer her. Cousins III asked some things about ghost rental that he already knew the answers to—due to his phone harassment of Chester during the past months. He could only hope Midi didn't know the deep details of all those calls. And, in fact, she did not.

When the food was gone and all that was left of the drinks were the melted remains of burnt-sienna goo, Cousins III at last dared his most daring question yet: "What did you want to see me about?"

He immediately regretted his audacity, because Midi didn't answer right away. She stared at him. Plopping her chin onto one fist, she narrowed her eyes at him and just stared at him for about a week, by his reckoning. Then she said, "About dinner," and stood up.

Fireflies were beginning to prickle the deepest shadows under trees with their wandering starlights. Midi stood contemplating them for a moment, hands in pockets, a plastic baggy of empty takeout containers hanging from one wrist—the largest and least colorful of her many bracelets. Then she reached out with her free hand and scooped a little buggy star out of the air. Curious, Cousins III approached her. Midi turned her hand thumb down and the firefly crawled up; she turned her hand thumb up and it reversed and still went up.

"Why does it climb up before it flies?"

Cousins III blinked. "Pardon?"

"There's nothing stopping it flying away anytime. Why does it feel like it needs to climb to the highest spot before it can open its wings?" The firefly was midway across her palm.

"It could go right now. What makes a firefly need to climb up as far as it can?"

"I don't know," Cousins III said, and he couldn't, realistically, have been happier. If someone had given him a magic lamp with a genie and three wishes, he'd have wished that Midi would call him up every day to go and eat indescribable substances and talk about the unusual choices made by bugs.

The firefly reached the top of Midi's thumb, considered a moment, and departed. Midi faced him abruptly. "I took the bus. Drive me back?"

"Of course. Gladly." They returned to the car, after disposing of their trash in the proper receptacles. Once there, Cousins III started the car—and the air conditioner—and realized: "Back where?"

"My office. I'll direct you." And she began by pointing him in the right direction. "It's where I'll be staying for the summer. Where the ghosts are, when they don't have work. I won't ask you in, though. If you want to meet the ghosts that's fine, but all at once would be a lot for you, I think." She glanced at him, a bit bemused. "You seem a little easily overwhelmed, sometimes."

Cousins III pondered this, while keeping his eyes studiously on the road, against all temptations. "At work, I'm not," he finally said. "At work I have a lot to do sometimes, but I just take care of it. Some people get overwhelmed, but I don't. But I guess with other things…" He glanced at her, briefly. "With some things, things I don't know much about…maybe I can be like that, a little."

Midi smiled and nodded. Then, with exaggerated gravitas, she said, "Climb up slowly. Climb a little higher, and when you reach the top, take flight." Her tone dropped back to normal. "You'll be fine. Okay look, coming up here on the right—but don't turn, just look—see where the dollar store is? This is the strip mall with my office in it. But we don't go in the front here. We go around the block and pull in the back. This road, take a right."

As directed, Cousins III passed the extremely disused strip mall and rounded a corner. The whole thing vanished from view behind a thick line of trees and some row houses. Another turn, and he thought he could see the dollar store's lights ahead in the twilight. They were on a one-lane, unmarked road that had been last paved sometime during the hair metal era. His GPS dinged at him, disbelieving his choices.

"Okay, we're behind the strip mall now. There's the turn into the back lot. Kill your headlights first." Feeling himself to be standing on the ragged edge of lawbreaking, Cousins III obeyed. "No, not toward the dollar store, the other way. All the way to the end. Yup, here we are!" Cousins III stopped where he was, seeing no markings for parking spaces. The act of a true renegade. Midi unbuckled and pointed. "So this unit at the very end here, this is us." Then she twisted around in her seat to face him and extended a hand, with only the smallest finger extended. "I swear you to secrecy now," she said.

Cousins III nearly shivered. Was this the fabled pinkie promise, of great solemnity to children and great cuteness when heroines of romantic movies did it? He blinked at Midi. She looked nothing like a heroine of a romantic movie. But as for cuteness, she could pile-drive every last one of them into a pink birthday cake.

He linked pinkies. Somewhere, William the Conqueror glowed with pride for his distant grandson.

Midi gripped his little finger and said, "Okay. You can't tell anyone. See, technically we're sort of squatters. I can't afford to rent this place. But like, it's empty, and mostly the ghosts just stay here, and it's sort of a given that no matter where ghosts go, they kind of always are squatters anyway, if you think about it. So it's not like anyone could evict them even if they knew."

Cousins III nodded, but had to observe, "They could evict you. If you're living here."

Midi winced. "Well, yeah. That's the part where we keep it hush-hush. My apartment gets *really hot* in summer and I can't afford to run the A/C and I can't live in that sauna, so I kinda camp out here during the bad weather. That's not so legal. And we are borrowing the phone line from the nearest business—that one—because he really doesn't use it. And we *kinda* siphon a little electricity to run a few things." She released Cousins III's hand and began to gather her phone and possessions. "That's the one I feel bad about, because he does have to pay for his power usage. There isn't much I can do to compensate him for that, but I try to send customers his way once in a while. Mostly on social media, which he doesn't even know exists. I updated all his business info in Google, or the internet wouldn't even know he's there. I even set up an email address for him and I keep an eye on it, in case any dingus-heads can't read the listed hours of operation or want to know if he has a certain book. What a ridiculous thing to ask! Like a real store owner has time to check his inventory for every curious cat who thinks of a title." Midi shrugged. "But I get a ghost to go over and look, and I answer for him. Sometimes I think it helps." She laughed. Cousins III grinned, without knowing why. "Jemmie told me one time a lady showed up and was all, 'Hello, I emailed you about Faulkner's *The Sound and the Fury*' and she expected him to have it at the desk for her or something. And he looked at her like she was a talking hamburger, because he has no idea what email is, and he pointed her to the right shelf. They were both so confused!"

Now Cousins III laughed, seeing the full comedy of the situation, and also because Midi was just talking so much and he thought that was ideal.

"Anyway, thanks for the ride, and now you know where Rent-a-Ghost is." She bounced out of the car, then leaned down and added, "Don't call Chester anymore, he doesn't like it. Just text me." Then she vanished, and Cousins III watched her raise the loading dock shutter and disappear inside. *I can text her*, he thought, and then: *What about?* She hadn't said. *Does she mean with business questions, or...?*

His phone buzzed. It was the start of a new thread: a text from Midi. It said, *Next time, not Lao's, until summer's over. Too hot. Someplace with A/C. You can pick if you want. Goodnight!*

Cousins III drove home safely, and that was saying a lot, given his attention deficits that night.

The ghosts, still gathered in the back room, looked up in spectral attention as Midi joined them.

Midi, for her part, kicked off her geta and dropped her backpack and fanny pack and surveyed the ghosts with her hands on her hips.

Chester broke the silence. "Well?"

Philosophically, Midi said, "Dead men tell no tales." Then she shrugged. "You were all right. Congratulations. I reward you with an hour of TV. My phone is fully charged."

A chorus of voices asked the same question in various ways:

"Did he declare himself?"

"Are you two an item?"

"Hast plighted thy troth?"

"How long is the engagement to be?"

"Does his family approve?"

"Did he confess?"

"He asked you out?"

And on the tail of these questions, half drowned by them, one other question:

"Seriously, what's troth?"

Midi waved her hands above her head. "*Ya!* The answer is *no*—Xerox that and pass out copies. I'm just saying you're right. I didn't say anybody's getting married."

"Oh, dash it all." Various other statements echoed this feeling.

Chester alone eyed her silently, until the chorus died away. Then he asked, "Do *you* like *him?*"

The intense curiosity in the room was transparent, as were the occupants. Midi raised her head high and proclaimed, "Maybe. But I'm going to climb a little higher before I decide to take off." Then, without admitting of further comment, she said, "Somebody fetch the kids, they won't want to miss the little TV."

7

In the before-time, Cousins III ate lunch at his desk. Once a week, he ate with co-workers. Occasionally, he ate with clients for business reasons. No one at the office could explain the sudden erratic preference for lunching out by himself.

Cousins III arrived at Everything Breadbowls promptly upon being summoned. Midi was already there, sitting with a middle-aged lady and two twenty-somethings. Cousins III decided not to interrupt. He sat down nearby and waited, listening with great interest.

The middle-aged woman was saying, "I understand the campers enjoy the haunted forest event, but I think it got a little out of hand last year. Some of the boys broke branches off some saplings, and one group even attempted to start a fire in the forest, *not* in the designated campfire spots, under supervision." She gave the two twenty-somethings two arched eyebrows of reproof. "We're going to have to keep it within camp regulations if we want to do it again this year."

One of the twenty-somethings quickly said, "The lack of supervision was our fault. We gave them very careful instructions, but you know how campers are. We've already planned out how to avoid the problems this year."

The other twenty-something added, "We think part of the problem was we used too big an area, which made it hard for us to keep counselors on all the groups. So we're going to cut things down to this section," and he indicated an area on a campground map.

Midi asked, "Does that mean you want to reduce your rentals this year?"

The first twenty-something said, "No no, I think that's another issue. We were thinking that silence and dark helps build tension, but it seems like the gaps between spooks were too long for the campers' attention span. So we're thinking of keeping the number of rentals the same, and just having them closer together on the haunted trail. Provided we can do that." She glanced at the older woman.

A nod. "I told you, the entertainment budget is the same, and it's up to you how you choose to spend it. If you want to use some of it for a haunted hike in the woods, that's your prerogative."

"Okay, great," Midi chimed in. "So if you want to change the locations, I'll need to come out in advance and survey the area before placement. The week before camp opens is still a good time, right?"

"Yes," the older woman said. "Our off-season construction project got pushed back to next year, due to the budget. The counselors will be there for team-building that week as usual."

"Awesome, so I can come out on Wednesday and you guys can run me through the area and we'll map out the placements, and then the day before the event I'll be there to set up?"

"Yes please."

"Great."

"Okay, then here's your contract to sign, all the same as last year, and the deposit is the same, and for your reference," she took out a paper and passed it over, "here's a list of the rentals from last year, so you can re-check. If you change your mind about the number or anything, just call me within a week. No cancellation fee within a week."

The middle-aged lady signed the contract and paid the deposit, and the counselors studied the list and pointed to their map, discussing together. Midi glanced over at Cousins III and smiled. Cousins III suffered a joy attack. Midi was looking like a beautiful collision of the Disney store and Hot Topic, and she had asked him to lunch, and Cousins III could not have been happier.

The meeting wrapped up, and Cousins III joined Midi at her table. "Hey! Sorry for the wait." He was shaking his head even as she continued, "I had these guys in the morning and another customer is coming in an hour and a half, so I figured I'd see what you were up to during my break."

"It's perfect. I needed to eat lunch anyway. Is this place good?"

Midi beamed. "The air conditioning is the *best!*" Then, with a shrug: "And yeah, the food is fine, but this is another one of those really overpriced places."

Cousins III seized the opportunity with the swift decision and magnificent courage that had made his ancestors such a success at Hastings. "Then let me buy you lunch? Anything you want."

Midi grinned. "You might regret that."

Cousins III found himself smiling along. "Try me."

Everything Breadbowls was aptly named. As it turned out, they served everything in breadbowls. Soups, of course, but also salads, pastas, even sandwiches—ingredients curiously arranged in a semi-open-faced style. They also served dessert breadbowls, employing a sweeter bread, often brioche. These were such as cinnamon roll breadbowls, various fruit cobbler breadbowls, vanilla almond granola breadbowls, s'mores breadbowls, banana bananabreadbowls (with Nutella), and pumpkin spice latte maple cream breadbowls. But Cousins III did not venture too deep into the menu's many notions.

Midi kept things on a fairly sane level and ordered a hot Italian sandwich in a breadbowl, a cinnamon roll in a breadbowl, and a frozen caramel latte. First, she gutted her cinnamon roll breadbowl of its nuts and spices and dumped them into her latte and mixed it up; then she transferred her Italian meats and cheeses and veggies and sauces, as best she could, into the brioche breadbowl; then she produced a little thermos shaped like a blue furry monster and poured what appeared to be SpaghettiOs® into the vacated ciabatta breadbowl. Upon her request, the bored teenager behind the counter microwaved it for her, only frowning slightly at the sight of what he may have guessed was not the soup of the day.

Cousins III had homestyle baked potato soup in a breadbowl and rustic apple cobbler in a breadbowl and coffee—in a coffee mug. Everything Breadbowls had lied a tiny bit—they did use cups for beverages.

Lunch for two was only $60—a real bargain, as far as Cousins III was concerned.

"So who did you rent to the summer camp?"

"Mmm," Midi swallowed, "some orbs—we start small and build up to the full apparitions—and a couple poltergeists, Doyle and Lulu. Then three of the ladies and Bobby. The campers take several different hiking trails and they won't encounter all the apparitions, but everyone should see at least one of them."

"The camp is a regular customer?"

"A repeat, yeah. Third year in a row."

"Ah. What about your next meeting?"

"Next is," Midi flipped a file open without putting down her sandwich-breadbowl, "a new one. Apparently this guy is a landlord, and one of his tenants hasn't paid rent in over a year and he wants them gone but they won't leave. I guess the legal process for evicting a tenant is incredibly slow and expensive, and he thought it would be cheaper and faster to just rent a ghost to haunt the place and scare the tenant out of the house."

Cousins III hummed thoughtfully. "I suppose it depends on the temperament of the tenant. It might not work; on the other hand, it might solve the problem instantly."

"Oh, I think it'll work." Midi grinned. "I'm giving him Polly. Nothing like a little girl ghost for creepiness. And Polly is relentless. Kids are like that—just nonstop. Plus I'm gonna offer him a poltergeist at half off to back her up. I have a good feeling about this customer. He's got quite a few rental properties. If this fixes his tenant problem quickly, he'll be back often."

"Your sales tactics are so clever," Cousins III said, carefully concealing his adoration.

Midi blinked, startled by the sudden overpowering beam of blatant adoration. Then she laughed a little and went back to her lunch.

Cousins III did not understand the mysterious laughter, but he thought it was utterly charming.

"Hey, you want to come with me when I go to the summer camp and map out the haunted hike?"

Cousins III's heart eclipsed its previous speed records. "Can I? Won't I be in the way?"

"Nah, you're fine. I don't mean when I'm placing the ghosts. I mean, you could, but it's really not interesting and it sometimes takes a while and you might get bored. But before that, I'm going out there to map out the hike with the counselors. Basically we'll just be going for a hike ourselves, and I make notes on the map."

Cousins III agreed immediately and offered to drive. "Oh yeah, you're rich! Great!" Midi's approval glowed within him.

Having never gone hiking before, Cousins III went to an outdoor sports store and made a salesman's day by buying everything he could possibly need for hiking in summer—though really, he'd have done fine with just a decent pair of boots and a large water bottle. Midi laughed at his over-preparedness. She was wearing a strawberry-patterned sundress and hiking boots, with a beer helmet carrying two water bottles and a lemon-yellow parasol she claimed was to keep the sun off, but Midi mostly seemed to use it for sneaking up on birds and squirrels and opening it suddenly at them.

Cousins III took charge of her map and pencil case and diligently made neat, clear little notes on it as indicated by the counselor guiding them. He found a wide selection of colored gel pens in Midi's pencil case and used them to color-code the marks and notes. Midi often stopped for brief conversations with the counselor about various possible haunting spots, none of which looked like anything spooky to Cousins III, but they were imagining the trail at night, which he was not really able to do. Still, he made himself useful and spent time with Midi, so it was worth taking off work early and mystifying the entire office with his inexplicable leave of absence.

And at Midi's invitation, he drove her back to Rent-a-Ghost and stopped a while to meet some of the residents.

"Most of them are out," Midi explained, hauling up the loading dock shutter, "so you can meet just a few of them and see the place without getting too overwhelmed. The ladies are all gone for the day, so it's just Chester, Lord Watley, Bobby, and Jemmie right now. Polly is rented, as you know, though not for much longer, and some of the poltergeists are around, but since they can't talk and you can't see them, you don't need to worry about them. Here we are." She grasped Cousins III's hand and pulled him up to the loading dock with wiry strength.

"Egad!" A portly gentleman in a waistcoat, tailcoat, top hat, and spats leapt nearly an inch at their appearance.

"That's Lord Watley—sorry, Lord Watley. You can go back to your moustache." Under her breath, she added, "He doesn't work much, except in October when I really need him. He's terrible at being scary." Then: "Ah, that's Bobby, who will be going to the camp."

A skinny and transparent young fellow grinned at Cousins III. "I get to make myself look like I was mauled by a bear, wanna see, dude?"

"Not now, Bobby, don't scare him."

"Midiiiiii!" A streak of pale light came through one wall, passed through Midi, and turned back to repeat its charge as Cousins III leapt aside.

"Jemmie, Jemmie, Jem-Jem, calm down, calm down. We have a visitor. Don't scare him, okay?"

"Ohhh...*him*." Jemmie pulled up short and regarded Cousins III. No longer a spectral typhoon, he immediately became a tiny sage whose deep thoughts were one with the universe.

"Him indeed," another voice said, and Cousins III looked around to see a pudgy fellow drifting down through the ceiling. "Midi," he added at once, "there were two telephone calls while you were gone." His ghostly tone was plainly plaintive.

"And that's Chester, you've met, sort of," Midi finished off with a gesture.

Cousins III had a quick existential crisis and then decided that he was just going to be okay with a certain amount of transparency among his new acquaintants and not think too much about it beyond that. The payoff was worth it.

"So this is it." Midi spread her arms, smiling. "This is the main area for us. The empty store is through there, the bathroom is there, and any other doors you see are storage of some kind, but we mostly stick around here. No windows to outside."

"And you're staying here for the air conditioning?"

Midi laughed. "No, because I don't *need* air conditioning here. I've got them!"

A nod. "It is quite chilly in here. That's them?"

"Great, huh?"

"Midi, the calls..."

"All right, Chester, all right." She smiled at Cousins III. "Work awaits. Summer is when business starts picking up a bit, after all. Thanks for driving me today."

"Not at all, I enjoyed the hike." Cousins III glanced around and gathered his Norman courage once again, as well as some of his old-world gentility. "It was very nice meeting you all." To Lord Watley: "Sorry for startling you." To Jemmie: "Thank you for not running through me." To Bobby: "I'm sorry, I'd rather not see anything horrific. But I'm sure you'll be great on the haunted hike." And to Chester: "Nice to finally meet you in person. Thanks for, um, all your help."

And last, with glad relief, to Midi: "I had a wonderful time. Please feel free to contact me whenever you wish. I'd love to buy you lunch again. Or dinner."

"Or breakfast?" She beamed.

Somewhat taken on the left foot by the question, Cousins III nevertheless had a ready answer. "Of course. I usually start work at nine, but before then I'm free. And I can go in late occasionally, as long as there isn't a meeting."

Chester observed, with ghostly amusement, some of the confusion plain on the man's face. Buying a girl lunch was one thing. It could be just friendly. If that was a date, it was a casual one. Buying her dinner was more of a date. The guy was trying. But he had no frame of reference by which to understand a breakfast date. What, he was clearly thinking, did *that* mean?

Chester did not offer any insight. He could have said, "Midi's favorite meal of the day is breakfast. A breakfast date is an upgrade surpassing dinner." He did not say anything. He smiled benignly and was unhelpful. This guy had annoyed the heck out of him with pointless telephone calls all through the spring. Not that Chester was holding a grudge. Chester *couldn't* hold a grudge; it was dangerous to try. But he could enjoy the man's befuddlement a little bit.

8

The dog days of summer saw Midi mostly hanging around the strip mall during the day and running out for rental meetings in the evening—sometimes late. She was filling up the schedule in advance of October. Her days and nights got a little tangled up. During the day, Cousins III was usually working, and Midi didn't want to go out anyway; in the evening, she was usually working. If they wanted to meet, they had to meet for breakfast.

Cousins III wanted very much to meet, so breakfast it was. Midi wanted very much to eat breakfast and avoid the heat, so breakfast it was, and early, too. Despite late working hours, she often met Cousins III at six in the morning to eat together. This left Cousins III with an hour or more to spare between breakfast and the start of his workday, so he began going to the gym with impressive regularity. His results were less impressive, but they were something, at least. Midi made up her lost sleep with naps in the middle of the day, bathed in free cold air. If the telephone rang, she woke at once and answered it.

Chester drifted above the abandoned end of the strip mall, just enjoying death—hardly any telephone responsibilities for months, and no miserable hot days ever again. No cold days either, for that matter, but between the two, Chester took Midi's view. He did not remember it well, but he knew that he used to get very sticky in the summer— and of course he lived long before air conditioning was invented, so he had no idea what it was even like to be able to adjust the temperature in one's home.

Most of all, he liked that now he could enjoy summer. He liked to just drift and admire the light, without being troubled by the accompanying heat. He studied the explosions of plant life that oozed over the edges of the parking lot and bubbled up through the crumbling crust of old tarmac.

Without the telephone to interrupt him, Chester could fix his gaze on a plant that took his fancy and watch it until he caught it growing. Thunderstorms and rain made the heat unbearable for skin-wearing folks; for Chester, it was all just a wonderful light show, and the resulting humidity gave the air a pretty haze. Most of all, he liked to look at things through the wavy heat rising from the parking lot, or from the hot metal roofs of cars, when any happened to be parked nearby for a while.

He liked to look at the world through the warp and wobble of the heat, or to stare straight up into a downpour until he felt like he was shooting through a thousand water-stars, or to catch a weed taking a moment to tilt a leaf a little sunward.

He did not like to answer the telephone, but Midi was around now, so at least for a while, he didn't have to.

Alas for the harried receptionist, summer's carefree days always come to an end. Midi moved back into her apartment when the heat broke in September, leaving the telephone to Chester again, and just at the busiest season. Poor Chester only wished to watch the leaves change color, but the telephone would always interrupt his autumnal reverie.

"I'm sorry, but our child ghosts are booked that weekend. ...Yes, already. ...Yes. ...No, I don't need to double-check. Our child ghosts are fully booked for October. ...August. ...Well, we have a gentleman ghost, and we have ladies. We can still do either old or young ladies, but if you want them you'd better reserve them now. ...An old lady? Okay, when can you meet the agent to sign the lease?"

Chester finally withdrew his head from the telephone with a pained seeming-sigh, then immediately frazzled around the edges at the sight of Lord Watley standing by, observing with a morose look. Chester re-collected his essence and gave Lord Watley an impatient look. "Haven't I asked you to at least clear your throat or something if you arrive when I'm in the telephone?"

Lord Watley continued in his tragic aspect. "I say old chap, I do think you might mention my title. It isn't as if every gentleman held a peerage."

Chester gave no proper awe to the critical matter of class. "Being a lord doesn't make you creepier or more likely to be rented. Anyway, your title now belongs to your great-grandson."

"But dash it all—"

"You'll still get work. Everyone works in October. Except me. No one ever books me, so I get to answer the telephone all year long." Chester gave Lord Watley a flat look. "If you want to be more in demand, learn to make yourself spookier."

Lord Watley gave his own pretense of sighing. "Right ho," he concluded, departing. He did not argue, because Chester had heard it all before: grotesqueries interfered with good grooming. That is to say, his moustache would fall from perfection if he made himself look a fright, and that, alas, Lord Watley could not seem to do.

Most of the ghosts were tactful toward those who were only booked as a last resort, when no one else was available. But Chester was the ghost who, as he said, was never booked at all, so he wasn't sympathetic at all.

Chester shoved his head back into the telephone. "...Midi, got another one for you." His voice crackled a bit over the line, like a bad connection.

Midi frowned. As Chester gave her the details, she flipped on speaker mode and glanced at her bars—all full. Then: "Okay, slow down—October what again?" She was hiking up the leg of her parachute pants to find a blank spot on her thigh to write on. Real estate tended to be scarce this time of year.

After ending the call, Midi thoughtfully returned her pen to her pocket protector. She was wondering if she needed to make time to stop by the strip mall and make sure everything was fine with the phone line. Her contemplations came jerking off their track, however, at the sound of a severe, "*Ahem!*"

"Oh!" Midi relaxed again at the sight of the stern specter in her doorway. "Is it that time again already?"

Mrs. Amelia Gladstone floated in with perfect poise, pointedly ignoring the inelegantly bare leg of her employer. She assumed her seated posture with twice the dignity, as though to overrule the indignity of Midi and her floor pillow. "I might observe, young lady," she began, "that a writing desk would not inconvenience you greatly, and you would find it a most serviceable addition to your..." A glance about. "Morning room."

"I'm good." Midi replaced her pant leg. "How's your haunting?"

But Mrs. Amelia Gladstone was not one to be lightly deterred from her theme. "I have observed that Mr. Smith, Sr. also owns one of those little black objects, and he occasionally uses it to take down memoranda. Perhaps you might do the same."

Midi glanced at her phone. "Why?"

Mrs. Amelia Gladstone gave her a long, pursed look. "It might be preferable to barbaric markings upon your person."

"Ah. I guess it might." Midi shrugged. "If you've got nothing to report..."

"I have no particular matters to discuss," Mrs. Amelia Gladstone cut in authoritatively. "However, I believe I must point out to you that the six-month rental term will be coming to a conclusion presently."

"Really?" Midi perked. "Hmm. Well, for business we want a contract renewal, but of course it's better for the old man if he doesn't need you around anymore, and the actual customer paying the bill is kind of a personal connection at this point, so I shouldn't bilk him..." Her voice lowered briefly. "Even if he *is* rich." Then, in her usual tone, Midi concluded: "Hum. I dunno what to do. I guess this is why you don't get involved with customers."

Mrs. Amelia Gladstone contributed a grave silence.

Midi picked her phone up, tapped it a few times, put it back down, and looked up at Mrs. Amelia Gladstone. "What do you think?"

"I beg your pardon?"

"About all this, I mean. He's your customer. Any suggestions?"

Raising her gaze to the far-away places where she could remember girls acting decently—which places appeared to be out the window, judging by the direction of her eyes—Mrs. Amelia Gladstone answered, "Mr. Smith, Sr. is much improved of late. However, whether he would continue so if his solitude were resumed is not a matter upon which I can speculate. It would be necessary for me to make a trial of the matter, perhaps by withdrawing some of the time and appearing with less constancy. I should advise you to discuss this matter with the grandson. But as far as where your business connections with him stand in light of your personal attachment, I cannot make any recommendation."

"Cool, super unhelpful, thanks."

Mrs. Amelia Gladstone bowed her head regally in acknowledgement.

Rather than press the point, Midi sat silent, tapping a swift tattoo with teal-sparkle false nails on her coffee table. Gaining nothing from this, she turned to the window for inspiration. Sadly, the land of memory, which Mrs. Amelia Gladstone found out there, filled with decorous young ladies, contained no help for Midi, who was not lacking in manners as far as she knew. Not wishing to overstay her welcome, Midi backed out of memory lane and threw herself into the first act of decision she had to hand.

She called Cousins III.

Cousins III was sitting through the winding-down summary part of a weekly planning meeting. When his phone buzzed, he glanced at it, then jumped to his feet. He nearly upset his chair, but did not. He definitely *did* upset the developer who had been speaking. "Excuse me," Cousins III mumbled. He also said, "Hello? Hang on a second," and, "Sorry, I need to take this," all in a jumble, leaving it to his various listeners to figure out which sentences were intended for them and which were not. At the same time, he was grabbing his phone and fleeing the startled eyes of all his team members.

Ensconced in the lavatory, Cousins III took a deep breath. "Hi," he said, and, "sorry about that, I was just getting out of a meeting."

"No problem," Midi said. She had succeeded in picking out which words had been meant for her. She was extremely competent in the realm of distracted conversation.

"It's past lunchtime. Did you want to get dinner?" Cousins III desperately tried to contain his tsunami of hope. He and Midi had met for lunch twice since the summer heat broke, but so far they hadn't had a proper dinner together. The first time, last spring, had been a chance encounter— and Midi hadn't even recognized him then, he plainly recalled—and the second time, in the park, surely could not be called a date. Cousins III was in ecstasies of suspense.

They were put to rest quite promptly. "Oh no, it's about your rental, actually."

"Huh? My r—oh."

"The original six-month term of your lease is almost up. Have you given any thought to whether you would like an extension or not?"

Cousins III's voice echoed desolately in the lavatory. "I don't know." Then, the tsunami of hope had another go at making landfall. "Maybe we should meet up and discuss my options?"

"Oh it's not that critical. We can talk about it next time I see you, if you don't know right now."

"Oh."

"Options are basically end contract, renew contract, or we can transition to a month-to-month pay-as-you-go, if you want to hold off a bit on the decision."

"…Oh."

"Just something to consider. That's all I had. See ya when I see ya!"

Cousins III looked down at his phone in a gloom, resenting the screen for showing him that "ended call" nonsense.

Midi said goodbye to Mrs. Amelia Gladstone, who would be back in two weeks for the verdict, unless she heard it from the customer himself first, during one of his visits. Then Midi gave a thought to the October schedule—and also a snack.

And Chester regarded the ringing telephone with ghostly loathing for a full half a minute, shadows of black gathering in his eyes. Then he smashed his head into the hated device and answered with: "No, nothing new since I called. …For Gladstone in October? Okay. I'll keep it in mind that she's an option. Is that all?" After a pause, he removed his head without a word of farewell. Without even asking what Midi was eating, though he could hear the telltale muffle of her words.

Midi blinked in confusion at the "ended call" screen, which was not having a red-letter day so far. No one liked the poor screen, though it was only doing its job. Then Midi studied her Pop-Tart® quizzically. Perhaps Chester did not like Pop-Tarts®? But how could he know it was a Pop-Tart®?

And Cousins III caught his developer on the way out of work and apologized for his abrupt departure from the meeting earlier. The developer said it was fine and he hoped nothing was wrong. Cousins III said no, of course everything was fine—and his expression and tone perfectly convinced the developer that someone close to his boss had died. The developer said that was good to hear, and he said it with deep sympathy and a pat on the shoulder, which mystified Cousins III.

9

October itself came and went in a whirl of autumn leaves and cheap plastic sheets hanging from trees with tinny microphones playing spook noises. The Acme Rent-a-Ghost company worked the whole month through. Midi was busier than anyone, running hither and yon to get contracts signed and deliver ghosts to their hauntings. But considering she meant to live off the profits for at least three months, she had no complaints.

Cousins III had elected to delay his decision and take the month-to-month contract, and he had also agreed to the suggestion that Mrs. Amelia Gladstone diminish her appearances, which was just as well, because Midi needed her. Few of the old ladies were as creepy as Mrs. Amelia Gladstone. So Mrs. Amelia Gladstone went out on short rental jobs, leaving Mr. Smith, Sr. to manage alone sometimes.

Cousins III was also alone a fair bit, because Midi didn't have much time for recreation. They still texted. It wasn't the same. Those little text bubbles simply did not express Midi, no matter what bonkers emojis she put in them. If Cousins III couldn't look at her and marvel at the latest fashion natural disaster happening in front of him, he couldn't be content. But he hadn't figured out how to ask her what she was wearing in a way that would represent his motives correctly. Text messaging was such a stone-age form of communication, utterly lacking in mutually understood nuance.

However, October could only last for 31 days, and not a day more. The post-Halloween lull began at last. There were still rentals—as Midi had said, things didn't really die out until January—but there was time for other things.

The loading dock shutter clattered as it raised, and Cousins III entered the back room of the strip mall on a chilly Saturday afternoon. Lord Watley paused in his ministrations to his moustache. "I say!"

Cousins III glanced around. "I know Midi isn't here yet; she's on her way. Is Chester here?"

"Oh, yes indeed, quite." Lord Watley indicated the storefront.

"Thank you." Cousins III opened the door leading forward.

He entered the empty store to find Chester with his head inside the telephone. His voice came from the device: "No sir, as I said, we don't rent demons. ...Because demons have malicious intent, and we can't possibly work with them. They're harmful."

Cousins III hesitated. Did ghosts see with their eyes? If they did, he supposed Chester couldn't see him right now.

"That's just not...even if we *did* rent demons, we couldn't possibly rent them to you just so you could exorcise them. It's a rental; you can't return it after destroying it! ...No, excuse me, but there's no such thing as a fake exorcism, not with a real demon... Well then why not just become a real exorcist?"

Glancing around, Cousins III tried to find a location that might make his presence more evident.

"...I see. ...I see. So you couldn't pass Latin. You do realize, don't you, that Latin is not the native language of demons? To them, it's a very modern language."

Unable to prevent himself overhearing, Cousins III paused at this new information. *Interesting. I wonder what language demons do speak?* Then he took into account what Chester was trying to convey to the would-be customer and decided, *Maybe it's not worth finding out. They probably wouldn't have anything nice to say, anyway.*

"No, I'm sorry, we don't have...yes I can see that. Yes, if something else pretended to be a demon, your fake exorcism would work fine, but I'm telling you that none of our ghosts look like demons or could possibly make themselves pass convincingly as a demon. Yes, I'm sure. Yes. Sorry about that, have a nice day."

With a groan, Chester emerged from the phone. Cousins III straightened and began: "I—"

At that, Chester's entire outline jumped like an audio waveform registering a quiet room in which a teenager suddenly began to express his deepest feelings on a drum kit. Cousins III jumped too—only vertically, though. He wasn't sure what he was looking at for a moment. Then Chester re-gathered his ethereal essence and glared at him. "I would *appreciate it,*" he said, with a strange sort of deep reverberation in his voice, "if you would make some sort of sound when you come in, if you see that I'm in the telephone. You even have a body! Scuff your feet or clear your throat or something!"

"I'm sorry. I'll remember. Um, Midi isn't here yet."

"*Clearly.*" Chester's translucent shape had become oddly shadowy and hard to see through. He did not seem eager for polite chit-chat.

Cousins III struggled within himself. Part of him felt highly disinclined to attempt conversation with an unfriendly dead person; the other part of him recalled that Midi had called Chester a friend, somewhat—certainly he was the one ghost entrusted with helping to run the business. And Cousins III was in that special emotional stage when the object of his interest, still so elusive as far as he knew, inspired a corresponding interest in anything and everything connected to herself.

In a word, Cousins III was made to woo, and his would-be woo-ee was absent. He must, therefore, woo her next of kin.

"I haven't seen a phone like that since I was a kid. You can't use newer ones?"

"*Mmm.*" Never had a vague hum been so definitive and firm.

"Have you ever tried to set up some kind of online scheduling system? Or at least a preliminary form people could submit?"

The dark and cloudy specter regarded him for a moment. "You are talking about that internet thing, aren't you?"

"Oh. Um, yes. I guess you don't use the internet?"

Chester appeared sullen, but some of his cloudiness began to dissipate. "I can't interact with it."

"But you can interact with the phone?"

Chester shot a venomous look at the offensive rotary. "Yes."

Cousins III pondered. "Okay—sorry, can you clear this up for me? Why can you use the phone and not a computer? As long as it plugs in and there's no battery to drain…"

Now mostly back to his usual transparency, Chester grudgingly explained. "It's not like I can operate things. Until all these electric inventions appeared, I couldn't interact with anything, really. But anything that's electric, I can turn it on by touching it. I can't really do anything else, though. I can turn on those internet things, but then they don't do anything." He paused. "If I try really hard, I can make them show a big mess of black and white speckles."

"Analog snow," Cousins III murmured. "Weird." Then he considered the rest of Chester's information. "So even if a mobile phone were plugged in constantly, you couldn't use it. Because it's already on, and you have to interact with it internally to do anything, like text or even answer a call."

The ghost shrugged his sloping shoulders. "Does it matter what kind of telephone it is? They all have obnoxious people inside them."

Cousins III pondered again, briefly. "So really, it's not the phone you hate, it's being a receptionist?"

"*Mmm.*" This hum broke the previous hum's world record for decisiveness.

"Then why are you the one who answers the phone?"

Alas for Chester, the answer that was generally known among the ghosts was entirely unknown to this living fellow. There was nothing to do but explain—or else rudely vanish without answering. But if Chester had been the sort of ghost who could bring himself to rudely vanish without answering, he probably would not have been stuck as a receptionist.

"Because," he declared, gathering all his essence together for strength and fortification, "I never get rented. There isn't anything else for me to *do*, because no one wants me, so I get to answer the telephone. And before you ask, no one wants me because I'm not scary and I can't make myself scary. I can't change my appearance, I can't imitate horrible wounds and maiming, I can't make my jaw hang open really far, I can't send my head rolling off by itself, and I can't...do that flickering thing, whatever it is. Midi called it 'glitching,' I think." He faced Cousins III and spread his arms a bit. "I'm just this. And this isn't scary. So I'm stuck talking to the living. Any other questions?"

"Um, no. I understand your point. Thanks."

Chester took that conversational lull as an opportunity to depart without being rude, technically, and he ascended through the ceiling and was gone. Cousins III found himself confronted with, essentially, what he perceived as an HR problem in Midi's business. If he had been Chester's boss, he'd have done a skills assessment and a goals and values interview to see if he couldn't find a better fit for Chester within the company. The ghost was clearly not thriving in his current position.

Then again, by Chester's own acknowledgement, it sounded as if he didn't have the entry-level skills needed in the haunting business. The obvious management answer to *that* problem was to see if he could give the employee some additional training, but Cousins III didn't know if one could teach a ghost how to look frightening, or how to go about it even if one could. Still, as a good manager, Cousins III abhorred the idea of letting the receptionist go. Chester had a lot of knowledge within his field, a good memory, and apparently some internal motivation that kept him at his post as Midi's receptionist, despite his discontent in the job. These were qualities that could not be taught and could be very hard to come by. The vice president in Cousins III would never fire such an employee if he could help it. He wanted to find a mutually beneficial solution to this situation.

Then again again, Cousins III reminded himself, this wasn't his company. He wasn't the boss; Midi was. And speaking of things which were not his:

From the back of the store, Cousins III heard the clattering of the loading dock door opening, and he abandoned Chester's work-related issues with joyous alacrity—perhaps not a mark in his favor as a company executive, but certainly understandable in a young suitor.

10

Mrs. Amelia Gladstone was presented with a dilemma.

Throughout October, she had taken on a number of short-term hauntings—weekends, parties, corn mazes, and so forth—which occupied her greatly. It was serendipitous, as she had also been placed on a month-to-month rental and asked to diminish her presence in Mr. Smith, Sr.'s life. Mrs. Amelia Gladstone was well able to manage all this.

However, after Halloween, she was no longer urgently needed elsewhere; yet her monthly contract had been renewed almost without comment. She was now presented with the task of merely absenting herself from Mr. Smith, Sr.'s awareness, yet she had nowhere else to be and nothing to do.

Mrs. Amelia Gladstone abhorred boredom. She had lived an active and industrious life—as well as an extremely proper one, naturally—and she endeavored to do the same in death. Ennui, her great nemesis in life, stalked her far beyond the grave. If any ever had cause to wonder that a personage such as Mrs. Amelia Gladstone allowed herself to be *employed* in such an undignified profession, they would no longer think it strange once they knew her motives better.

It was also somewhat disturbing to her equanimity to be put in such an irregular position as a live-in rental without a set term. She was in all other ways perfectly satisfied with Mr. Smith, Sr., who was a quiet gentleman of decent breeding for one who had apparently spent his life in trade. His house met her conditions, and the work suited her sense of propriety uncommonly well. Despite all this, Mrs. Amelia Gladstone was not hoping for the rental to continue. She appeared harsh to indecorous young people, but she prioritized the good of others, and it was not particularly good for Mr. Smith, Sr. to go on indefinitely believing that his wife was still with him.

Considering all this, Mrs. Amelia Gladstone made several trips to her employer's lodgings, yet without meeting Midi. The flibbertigibbet seemed rarely to be home, these days. Mrs. Amelia Gladstone felt that discussing her contract with the grandson directly would be taking a liberty; but when she could not reach Midi after several attempts and the Christmas season was already upon them, Mrs. Amelia Gladstone decided to try what she might to advance matters and bring the rental to some sort of conclusion.

In the interests of which, she chose an evening when Cousins III was paying his grandfather a visit. When old Mr. Smith, Sr. went to the lavatory, she manifested visibly, as a polite warning, and then addressed his grandson.

"Young man, I wonder if I might make a request of you."

Cousins III, who had only jumped a little bit upon her appearance, said, "Oh, of course. What is it?"

Mrs. Amelia Gladstone restrained her feelings, though she longed to point out that *'How may I be of service to you, madam?'* would have been far more appropriate. "I would like to speak with Midi, but I have been experiencing some difficulty in contacting her. I understand you are able to do that. Would you be so kind as to notify her that I wish to speak with her at her earliest convenience?"

"Sure, no problem."

Again bearing up in the face of such a lack of gallantry, Mrs. Amelia Gladstone said, "Thank you." Then she faded from sight and settled herself to observe until the visit concluded.

Cousins III tapped his fingers on his little obsidian platter, which Mrs. Amelia Gladstone understood to be a communication device. She felt confident that he was corresponding with Midi, for when the little thing made a short hum, he smiled in a way that lacked all subtlety and tapped some more. He almost failed to notice his grandfather's return, so absorbed was he.

Midi, as it turned out, happened to be in the area, just getting out of signing a contract. Since Cousins III had reproduced Mrs. Amelia Gladstone's message verbatim, Midi interpreted "at her earliest convenience" to mean the matter was urgent, so she hopped on her scooter and went directly to Mrs. Amelia Gladstone's haunting location. This was not a problem at all, because Midi was thoroughly bundled up. Even the occasional snowflake failed to trouble her drive.

Upon arrival, Midi saw the black Lexus parked outside and realized Cousins III was here too, which he hadn't mentioned over text. Midi beamed happily, and without thought or hesitation, she rang the bell. After a minute, Cousins III appeared, then gaped at her. "Hi! What does Gladstone want?"

"Oh!" Cousins III shuffled back quickly. "Um, won't you come in? I'm not sure where she is just at the—"

"Toddy, is someone there?" an elderly voice called.

Midi made a brow-furrowed laugh and said, "Toddy?"

Cousins III was plunged into an abyss of indecision.

Here was Midi—his joy abounded.

On the other hand, here was Midi, and here was his grandfather. Midi needed to talk to her ghost; he couldn't shove her outside and send Mrs. Amelia Gladstone to talk to her out in the street. It was snowing! He *had* to ask Midi up to the sitting room. But that meant he had to introduce Midi to his grandfather—Midi in her giant neon pink parka with leopard print fur lining and bright yellow plaid snow pants and pale blue goggles and a lime green scarf with monster hands on the ends and black lipstick and cat-paw mittens.

It also meant he needed an explanation for who Midi was, how he knew her, and what she was doing here right now. Cousins III had none of these things. He had nothing much at all, really, except a mind-erasing happiness to see Midi so unexpectedly.

"Won't you—"

Midi was already on her way. Cousins III followed her into the room where his grandfather was sitting—and Mrs. Amelia Gladstone, unbeknownst to them all, for she was presently invisible and observing the scene with feigned disinterest.

"Hi! I'm Midi, nice you meet you! You must be Mr. Cousins Warwick Smith, Sr." Midi yanked off a mitten and extended a hand.

Mr. Smith, Sr. kindly took and shook it, saying, "I am. Do you know my grandson?"

"Oh yes, I'm here because he texted me." Midi did not elaborate on the subject further. Cousins III continued to scramble around in his empty mind for some explanation.

"Ah. He asked you to come?"

"Yep."

"Oh I see. I must have forgotten you mentioning it to me, Toddy. Then, why…?" Mr. Smith, Sr. glanced between them, lost his own thread for a moment, and then found a new one as Cousins III writhed internally, panicking. "Are you a friend of my grandson?"

Midi smiled brightly. "Oh, no. I'm his girlfriend!"

Had the floor been made of cheap modern materials, it would certainly have fallen out from under Cousins III at this moment. As it was, the floor was hardwood—a rich, lovely maple—and held up to the world-shattering news, in keeping with its 100 percent satisfaction guaranteed 30-year warranty.

"Oh my," Mr. Smith, Sr. said.

Mrs. Amelia Gladstone did not say anything, but she arched an invisible eyebrow in a most pointedly reproving manner.

Cousins III lurched slightly under the shock. As noted, it wasn't the floor's fault; the lack of balance was entirely his own problem. The maple flooring had not wobbled a bit. It was as stoic as Mrs. Amelia Gladstone in the face of this revelation.

"You are...dating my grandson?" Mr. Smith, Sr.'s voice was weak with amazement.

"Of course," Midi cheerfully confirmed.

"Since when?"

Midi blinked in surprise, turning toward Cousins III, from whom the question had come. "What do you mean 'since when'? After all this time, and breakfasts together, and...oh wait." Midi's eyes clicked up to the ceiling, which she seemed to study for a moment. She was not actually studying the ceiling, she was searching her memory—which was a shame, because it was a good ceiling, too. No flimsy gypsum drop-ceiling tiles in this house.

Midi blinked at Cousins III. "...Haven't we made it official yet?"

Cousins III was all agape. "...No?"

Thus confirmed, Midi burst into a sudden laugh. She turned to Mr. Smith, Sr. "Wow, I'm sorry, things have been kinda hectic lately with work and all. I guess we sort of skipped that chat. But anyway, we've been dating for a while. I'm glad to finally meet you!"

Mr. Smith, Sr. turned to Cousins III. "Is this true, Toddy?"

"Honestly, 'Toddy'? What's *that* from?"

"Some family joke from when I was a toddler," Cousins III breathed automatically. Then: "Are we really dating?"

Midi blinked at him like she was starting to worry about his sanity—a frequent concern, for her. "Well, yeah! I mean, we like each other and we meet up all the time. What else would you call it?"

Cousins III swallowed hard enough to send his Adam's apple vanishing right down under the collar of his shirt. "We like each other? So you...like me?"

"Oh my." Midi turned to Mr. Smith, Sr. and said, "'Scuse me a second." Then she attached one mittened hand and one bare hand to the flushed cheeks of Cousins III and applied a firm smudge of her own black lipstick to his hitherto unadorned lips.

Mrs. Amelia Gladstone heartily disapproved of this shocking display.

Mr. Smith, Sr. was startled, was aware that he ought to be either delighted or furious or something, and was mostly just baffled.

Cousins III wasn't anything that could be described, at least until Midi released him.

"Yes, so anyway, sorry for the mix-up and the surprise and all that. I'm just finishing the busiest season of the year for my business and like I said, it's been a bit crazy."

"Ah. Ehm…what business is that?" Mr. Smith, Sr. gathered himself, aided by the comfortingly mundane topic.

"Rentals!" Midi beamed, flopping into a seat and beginning to work her way out of her excessively warm outerwear.

Mr. Smith, Sr. nodded. "So you are a landlord?"

"Oh no, not property rental. Mmm, more like specialized equipment?"

"I see. And there is a busy season in your field?"

"Oh yes—early to mid-fall, mostly, but really the entire second half of the calendar year is when I do the most business. After the new year things will be dead for a while, but I have all that planned for. I guess this year I'll use my free time to make sure my boyfriend knows he has a girlfriend now!" And she laughed at herself, and Mr. Smith, Sr. couldn't help smiling. He had some reservations about this odd-looking girl-shaped whirlwind, but she seemed to have good business acumen. Her smile was also infectious.

Cousins III had not contributed much lately. He had not even managed to sit down. Nor had he attended to his black-smudged mouth, which looked ridiculous. Inside the little skin surrounding Cousins III too much was happening. All the fireworks in China for the Chinese New Year were exploding at once; all the hurricanes in the Caribbean from June to November were going Category 5 together; and under all that, the happiest little flower in the world was opening its petals to the sun and saying, "Hi. I'm here now. Everything is wonderful."

Needless to say, Mrs. Amelia Gladstone felt that the entire matter from front to back had not been handled with any propriety at all, but these were degenerate days, alas. The result was at least acceptable—the young people had an understanding between them and the approval, probably, of the family. Now if only Mrs. Amelia Gladstone could attract her employer's attention long enough to discuss her business matters.

However, as anyone might expect, Midi had entirely forgotten why she had come there, and she had no one to remind her. Mr. Smith, Sr. did not know, Mrs. Amelia Gladstone knew but could not mention it aloud, and Cousins III was a lost cause entirely. He did nothing useful for the remainder of Midi's visit. She talked a little with his grandfather while he grinned like an idiot, and when the visit seemed sufficient for an introduction and she took her leave, he offered to see her out.

Mrs. Amelia Gladstone followed, hoping to catch a word with Midi, but she returned to the parlor quickly. Cousins III, it seemed, was attempting to return the smudge of black lipstick to Midi, and instead was acquiring a good deal more of it for himself.

11

Christmas was in the air, and the entire world was blissful with anticipation, except for the rest of the world, which was having a stress-induced meltdown, but nobody minded them, because they weren't very aesthetically appealing. Happy couples went ice skating and shopping and looked at pretty lights and generally forgot to pay much attention to workaday things like customer complaints. And that was why Chester's caller had called back.

"Look, I'm sorry she didn't return your call, but you need to give her more than a day, and calling me won't do you any good. I don't handle the rental contracts, and—"

Some tinny noise came from the rotary telephone with most of a ghost sticking out of it. Two little pairs of ghostly eyes peeked through the back wall, but they couldn't make out what the caller said. Just as well. It wasn't fit for little ears, even intangible ones.

Chester's voice grew a notch tenser. "You were told *repeatedly* that he wasn't actually Charles Dickens. I know I told you, and it was in the contract you signed. He died in 1920 at the age of 45—that's as close as we get, and you agreed to that when you rented him."

The eyes and noses disappeared for a moment, and Jemmie and Polly turned their heads to look at Lord Watley, whose moustache was looking a little droopy, like dry-ice smoke trying to trickle to the ground.

Polly looked at Jemmie. "Is he in twouble?"

Jemmie reassured her, loud enough to be heard by Lord Watley. "It's not his fault. He did like normal and they told the customer already. Midi'll settle it."

Polly fretted. "But Midi in't here."

Jemmie had nothing to say to this, and they both poked back through the wall a bit to observe.

"No! No, why should we give you a refund? You signed a contract, and our ghost did what you wanted to the best of his ability, and we told you exactly what his abilities were and you agreed. ...I don't *care* about authenticity in your art! You run a local theatre—nothing you do is authentic, it's all illusion! You already got a real ghost and we *told* you he wasn't actually—"

"Oh no." Jemmie and Polly vanished into the back room again. "Jemmie, you see that?"

Jemmie nodded.

"What'd you see, squirt?" Bobby floated forward.

"Chesser's eyes is all black!" Polly looked like she might start crying.

Jemmie looked frightened. "We gotta get Midi," he said.

"Oh, I say!" Lord Watley expressed his consternation with a slight case of the vapors. His form became foggy and wafted floor-ward.

"Crap," Bobby said. "We don't know where she's at. Probably on a date somewhere, but who even knows?"

"We must make every effort to locate her," a stern voice interjected. The ghosts looked up to see Mrs. Amelia Gladstone sweeping in through the back wall. "I am able to inform you that she was calling upon my customer until recently, but she and her gentleman have departed, and I do not know their destination. Polly," she commanded, "you go to Midi's residence. Jemmie, you have been to my customer's house—don't lie, child, I know it was you—so you go there.

They may happen to return. Bobby, I want you to go inform the ladies. They know all the shops in this town extremely well. Appraise them—"

"Huh?"

"—*Tell* them the situation is urgent. Midi must come here at once."

"Okay, gotcha. Cool." Bobby streaked out of the strip mall.

"What about the boyfriend's house?" Jemmie asked. "What if they went there?"

Mrs. Amelia Gladstone looked graver than her own headstone. "None of us has been to his residence, not even I. We do not know where it is. If they have gone there, we shall not find them, and I fear Chester will be lost to us."

Lord Watley, who had been about to come around, returned to his vapors. The children looked dreadfully worried, and both streaked out of the strip mall in search of Midi. Mrs. Amelia Gladstone did not trouble herself with resuscitating Lord Watley—she had no smelling salts, and he couldn't have smelled them anyway. He must come together again on his own. Mrs. Amelia Gladstone went to the door separating the storefront from the back room. It was closed, as always, so she took up her station unobtrusively partway through it.

"Oh, you think so? Well if you want to know what *I* think about your stupid dinner theatre, I'll—"

Mrs. Amelia Gladstone frowned, but not at the uncultured speech she was unhappily privy to. The blackness in Chester's eyes had spread, and his entire form was darkening, like a clear glass of water into which someone had begun to pour ink. He was becoming shadow.

There was nothing Mrs. Amelia Gladstone could do, really. Hers was not the most soothing presence at the best of times, as she well knew. At present, Chester was in the telephone, and Mrs. Amelia Gladstone could not attract his attention without startling him, which would no doubt make matters worse. Still, she waited and watched. If he broke off the conversation and left the telephone, she would do her very best to calm him down. It was only proper.

The city's residents were busily preparing for Christmas, and for most of them, that was all they had really planned for that day—go about life as usual and work on their holiday prep. No one had expected to be jump-scared by a ghost at Macy's, but such is life—filled with the unexpected.

Unfortunately, ghosts under stress experience a heightened energy resonance, making them far easier to see, even in the light—not full sunlight, but fluorescent indoor light, certainly. A ghost can still master itself and maintain invisibility, even under stress and in low light, but the skill requires concentration. Once Bobby caught up with the ladies and told them the situation, they were in such a distraction and panic that they gave no thought to their visibility and went scattering over the city in a frantic search.

With glad luck, it was a bright, sunny December day, so even panicky ghosts were still invisible outdoors; thus, the ladies did not cause any traffic collisions. On the other hand, the indoor accidents more than compensated for the comparative road safety. It was a dark day for coffee. The latte losses were off the charts. More lattes were dropped on the floor with a startled scream, that day, than had been lost in the last three months combined.

In the face of this great tragedy, let the reader be consoled by remembering what was achieved. Most of the city's residents didn't know it—they mourned their lattes without consolation—but one of the ladies did, in fact, manage to find Midi and Cousins III having lunch together. When Midi heard what was happening, she grabbed Cousins III and raced to his car, urging him to drive to the strip mall as fast as he could.

Since it was his lady's command, Cousins III gave his very life for queen and country: he sped through yellow lights.

Mrs. Amelia Gladstone heard the clattering and noise of the living humans' arrival. She slipped away from her watchpost and met Midi racing through the back room.

"How is he?" Midi panted.

"Very far gone, I fear," Mrs. Amelia Gladstone said. "Do hurry. It may already be too late."

Even as she spoke, Midi was already rushing through to the store front. Cousins III belatedly jumped forward to follow her.

He very nearly crashed into Midi as he burst through the door behind her; she was locked in place, her expression stricken. "Chester..." she whispered, and then Cousins III understood.

The thing in the empty store didn't look anything like the Chester he remembered. It didn't look anything like any of the ghosts. It was all black, like living midnight, like tar gone to chaos. Its eyes were wild with ragelight, and it made a sound like the screaming of a thousand angry telephone bells.

"Chester!" Midi shouted over the noise. "Chester, calm down! Chester, please, please calm down!"

The thing thrashed and screamed, and Midi's eyes filled with tears. Cousins III felt a mighty knightly need arise in him to protect her and remove all her sorrows.

"Chester, don't do this," she begged. "What would I do without you?"

At this, the thing screamed horribly, swelling and tearing at anything near. Cousins III pulled Midi back as an old pile of rubbish went flying. The plea had only infuriated him further, and Cousins III suddenly guessed why.

"No more phones!" he shouted, and just to be sure Chester heard him, he repeated quickly, "No more phones! You won't need to answer the phone anymore! I have a plan. You never, never need to use the phone again!"

The chaos stilled somewhat at his words; the ringing shriek faded. Burning eyes roamed, found Cousins III, and fixed upon him. There was still nothing of Chester in evidence, but the thing was listening.

Suddenly on the spot, Cousins III glanced nervously at Midi, hoping he wasn't being too forward in her business. "I talked to Gladstone about it. She thinks my grandfather would be okay without my grandmother's ghost now, but he still has problems being alone." He made a tentative step toward Chester. "I was going to ask Midi about renting a ghost who could just stay with him for company. Like a roommate. Talk to him and just be there so he's not lonely all the time."

The black mass shrank slightly.

"You could do that, right?" Cousins III was cautiously encouraging. "No answering phones, no talking to customers. Just spend time with my grandfather. You'd have a permanent position haunting his house. You're the perfect ghost for the job. I really don't want to scare him; I just want someone to sit with him, watch TV, maybe go for walks on a nice day—you know, for his health." The black mass shifted into a distinctly Chester-like shape, and the horrid void of darkness began to fade, like a poster that had been hanging in the sun for years. "Could you consider taking the job?" Cousins III pressed. He felt Midi squeeze his hand. His ancestors' courage flooded him. "Gladstone—" A throat-clearing sound from behind him somewhere caught Cousins III. "I mean, Mrs. Amelia Gladstone can't keep pretending to be my grandmother forever. And my grandfather can't keep imagining that my grandmother is still with him. It's not healthy. You would be *so much better* at this. What do you say? Chester?"

"Yes, Chester, you can do it!" Midi eagerly chimed in. "And I won't ever call you for reports or anything. We'll talk when I'm visiting with Cousins number Three. The rest of the time, you just talk to Mr. Smith, Sr. And!" She beamed at her own stroke of genius. "He has years and *years* of old TV shows recorded!"

Chester, now only a little bit cloudy inside his ethereal essence, blinked and said, "Does he have *Friends*?"

Midi sniffled, tears on her happy face, and now it was Cousins III's turn to squeeze her hand. "Every. Single. Episode. I promise."

EPILOGUE

A certain ghost once visited the Rent-a-Ghost offices for a while—not to stay or to work, but simply to rest briefly from his travels. This ghost was a bit of a dramatist, and in the course of conversation with him, Chester asked him why it was such a rule that comedies must always end in weddings. This ghost looked confused and said that wasn't a rule at all; but Chester made his case by citing a number of the ghost's own works and pointing out that by pattern rule, *quod erat demonstrandum*, so to speak.

The visiting ghost blinked at this and thought for a while, and then said, in excellent modern English, "Well, you know how people always sort of sigh at the end after laughing very hard? I suppose it is like that. You wouldn't want to cut off a laugh in the middle. It might unbalance the humors."

"So the wedding at the end is a happy sigh for the story?" Chester evaluated this suggestion.

"In a sense," the ghost answered. "And also, I think, because if you keep the energy too high—that is, if the audience is laughing wildly right to the end—you run a greater risk of having rotten fruit thrown at you. Not in any disapproving spirit, you understand, but simply as an expression of their enthusiasm."

"I had no idea," Chester said. He was impressed by the old ghost's copious experience.

Thus, in the interests of ensuring that all expired food products make it safely into garbage disposals and compost:

Most people would put considerable thought and time into the types, colors, and arrangements of flowers for their weddings. Midi did not bother with flowers at all. She arranged spirit orbs. The effect was lovely, for the wedding was an evening one of necessity. Most of the guests couldn't make an appearance during the day.

Midi's primary difficulty during the planning was that half of her guests were ghosts, and the other half were alive and not quite prepared to sit through a ceremony with a bunch of see-through people. Originally, she wanted to just register and forget the rest, but Cousins III had certain obligations as the Vice President of product development at ZyTech Industries, and it would have been bad corporate manners to get married secretly and not invite anyone from work.

So.

As everyone knows, if they have ever heard a ghost story in their life, ghosts are, in fact, capable of appearing solid, at least for a while. As any thinking person might guess, assuming the guise of flesh is not easy, and it requires a massive amount of energy, which drains quickly. Midi did not think it would make for a pleasant wedding if half the guests vanished about two-thirds of the way through it, leaving the other half in shock and panic.

Fortunately, thanks to the age of mobile technology, everyone has a smartphone.

All Midi had to do was dispense with the seating tradition of bride's guests on one side and groom's guests on the other. After spending the day at Best Buy, her ghosts were all powered up enough to look alive for arrivals, and the wedding hall ushers had instructions to seat each of the bride's guests next to one of the groom's guests—between two of them, if possible. The ghosts were thus able to keep their energy up for the duration.

A few of the living guests thought the people sitting next to them were very quiet—no rustling of clothing or noisy breathing. No scent of perfume or cologne. Perhaps a tendency to sit just a pixel or two closer than necessary. But no one jumped to the notion of "ghosts." And every last phone battery was utterly dead by the end of the wedding.

At the reception, all the outlets were crowded with chargers, and the preppers who always brought a charger with them were the ones who got to take all the pictures. They were also popular among the bride's guests and made many new acquaintances that evening, none of whom they ever saw again.

As for Cousins III, he was a good groom who did as he was told and thought all Midi's ideas were wonderful. He didn't care if the reception hall looked like a thrift store display, and he thought all the music choices were perfectly appropriate as long as Midi liked the song. Most importantly, of course, he was prepared for anything when it came to what Midi would choose to wear for her wedding. Cousins III wore a perfectly normal tux, but he would have worn anything from a diving suit to a cowboy costume if Midi wanted him to. If she came down the aisle in a tutu, he would just be happy she was coming down the aisle to marry him.

This he repeated to his family more than many times. He did not want anyone casting funny looks at his bride, who would be the most beautiful girl in the world whether she wore sweats or jeans or an electric purple space invader suit.

To his amazement, Midi wore a white wedding dress.

Cousins III did not know what a hanbok was, nor that Midi's mother was more than a little involved in the dress choice. He noticed that the skirt was very big and fwoofy, but he was too busy bursting into snotty red-faced tears at the sight of her to deeply analyze the style of the traditional Korean dress.

Midi, for her part, was beaming and dragging her step-dad down the aisle to the tune of "I Got a New Way to Walk."

To imagine that Mrs. Amelia Gladstone *entirely* approved would be hoping for a bit too much. The proper ends were achieved, but she had never felt that the ends justified the means. Yet rather than "speak now," she held her peace—though she made no promises that she would do so forever.

As Chester suggested: "Save it for another century. For now, just let them be happy."

Mrs. Amelia Gladstone supposed she could live with that. Or rather, not *live*, of course, but—well, you know.

ABOUT THE AUTHOR

TC Fitzgerald is the prototype product of a small independent people farm on the East Coast of the United States. She is completely normal and not interesting at all.

Made in the USA
Las Vegas, NV
17 December 2024

14435995R00098